The Skeptic's Guide to the Great Books

Grant L. Voth, Ph.D.

PUBLISHED BY:

THE GREAT COURSES
Corporate Headquarters
4840 Westfields Boulevard, Suite 500
Chantilly, Virginia 20151-2299
Phone: 1-800-832-2412
Fax: 703-378-3819
www.thegreatcourses.com

Copyright © The Teaching Company, 2011

Printed in the United States of America

This book is in copyright. All rights reserved.

Without limiting the rights under copyright reserved above,
no part of this publication may be reproduced, stored in
or introduced into a retrieval system, or transmitted,
in any form, or by any means
(electronic, mechanical, photocopying, recording, or otherwise),
without the prior written permission of
The Teaching Company.

Grant L. Voth, Ph.D.
Professor Emeritus
Monterey Peninsula College

Professor Grant L. Voth earned his B.A. in Philosophy and Greek from Concordia Senior College in 1965. He received his M.A. in English Education from St. Thomas College in 1967 and his Ph.D. in English from Purdue University in 1971.

Professor Voth taught at Northern Illinois University, Virginia Polytechnic Institute and State University, and Monterey Peninsula College. He is Professor Emeritus in English and Interdisciplinary Studies at Monterey Peninsula College, from which he retired in 2003. He was the Monterey Peninsula Students' Association Teacher of the Year and also the recipient of the first Allen Griffin Award for Excellence in Teaching in Monterey County. For several years, he was a consultant for the National Endowment for the Humanities, reading proposals for interdisciplinary studies programs and advising colleges that wished to initiate such programs; he was also a National Endowment for the Humanities Fellow at the University of California, Berkeley. He served as director of an American Institute of Foreign Studies program for a consortium of California colleges in London in 1988, and he has led travel-study tours to England, Ireland, France, Greece, Turkey, and Egypt. He has been taking students to the Oregon Shakespeare Festival and the Santa Cruz Shakespeare Festival for many years, and he has been a frequent guest lecturer at the internationally acclaimed Carmel Bach Festival in Carmel, California.

Professor Voth is the author of more than 30 articles and books on subjects ranging from Shakespeare to Edward Gibbon to modern American fiction, including the official study guides for many of the plays in the BBC *The Shakespeare Plays* project in the late 1970s and early 1980s. He created a series of mediated courses in literature and interdisciplinary studies for the Bay Area Television Consortium and the Northern California Learning Consortium, one of which won a Special Merit Award from the Western

Educational Society for Telecommunication. This is Professor Voth's third course for The Great Courses. His first was *The History of World Literature*, and his second was *Myth in Human History*.

Table of Contents

INTRODUCTION

Professor Biography i
Course Scope 1

LECTURE GUIDES

LECTURE 1
A Skeptic's Way; Gogol's *Dead Souls* 4

LECTURE 2
Orwell's *Down and Out in Paris and London* 9

LECTURE 3
Cisneros's *The House on Mango Street* 15

LECTURE 4
Warren's *All the King's Men* 21

LECTURE 5
Kushner's *Angels in America* 26

LECTURE 6
Didion's *Slouching towards Bethlehem* 32

LECTURE 7
Bulgakov's *The Master and Margarita* 38

LECTURE 8
Zusak's *The Book Thief* 44

LECTURE 9
James's *Death of an Expert Witness* 50

LECTURE 10
Le Carré's *The Spy Who Came In from the Cold* 56

Table of Contents

LECTURE 11
Moore and Gibbons's *Watchmen* 62

LECTURE 12
Skeptics and Tigers; Martel's *Life of Pi* 69

SUPPLEMENTAL MATERIAL

Glossary 74
Biographical Notes 77
Bibliography 82
Credit 90

The Skeptic's Guide to the Great Books

Scope:

In 12 half-hour lectures, this course looks at some viable alternatives to those works that invariably wind up on a list of great books or in someone's literary canon or that can be purchased monthly in identical deluxe-bound volumes until one achieves the requisite 10 or 12 feet on the library shelf. There is, of course, nothing wrong with these books: They have stood the test of time and are the books we all know that we *should* read if we wish to think of ourselves as cultured or educated or well read—and our friends who are these things seem to have read all of them. The problem with them is that many of them are so massive that they are difficult to lift—let alone read—and we wind up daunted even before we begin. Others are extraordinarily difficult, requiring several years of preparatory study or an equal length of time in absorption of the works themselves in order to master them, which makes the prospect of undertaking them seem more an onerous duty than a pleasure. For these and other reasons, we keep putting them off for another time—a time that is always, like the horizon, a receding distance away—feeling increasingly guilty and experiencing twinges of anxiety every time we dust them.

This course invites you on a vacation from all of that to absorb some books that offer many of the same satisfactions as do the great books but without the pressure. The books of this course contain epic journeys and adventures in the great cities of the world; stories of growing up, initiation, and participation in important moments in the history of the world and individual countries; thoughtful analyses of important social and cultural movements and journalism that helps us remember and understand our own times; tales about contact with God and the devil; stories about crime and espionage and an account of a possible ultimate Armageddon in a parallel world; and tales of war and rumors of war. All of this is managed by a dozen authors who can keep us engaged as we read by teasing us and making us laugh (and sometimes cry) while teaching us about the human condition, just as do the authors of the great books—but usually in fewer pages and with a little less complexity, and with no guilt at all, because we are reading these not because we think we should but because we choose to. In the last lecture of this course, Terry Eagleton is cited to the effect that it is possible that what constitutes "literature" is less some quality that inheres in a text than as a way of reading it and that, in many ways, we create literature by the way we read. That is partly the idea of this course: By using the same techniques and analytical tools on these alternate authors as we would on those from the literary canon, we can receive many of the same benefits and pleasures. Perhaps we can even dare to begin new personal canons for ourselves.

Each of the first seven lectures will address one writer and relate him or her to a canonical work he or she is being considered in lieu of. For example, the first lecture, after dealing with a few items about canons generally, will analyze Nickolay Gogol's *Dead Souls* as an alternative to a work that is on everyone's great books list: Leo Tolstoy's *War and Peace*. The second will treat George Orwell's *Down and Out in Paris and London* as something we can read instead of F. Scott Fitzgerald's *The Great Gatsby* in terms of the part of the population it focuses on—and instead of Jonathan Swift in terms of the question of how far factual data can be manipulated and distorted and still be considered journalism or fact-based reporting. In the third lecture, we will consider a modern version of a Bildungsroman (a novel about growing up) in Sandra Cisneros's *The House on Mango Street*, comparing and contrasting it with books written by everyone's favorite author of such works, Jane Austen—particularly *Emma*. Next comes Robert Penn Warren's *All the King's Men*, based loosely on the career of Huey Long in Louisiana but using many of the same techniques as those of Joseph Conrad from the canon—particularly his *Lord Jim* and *The Heart of Darkness*. Tony Kushner's *Angels in America* will be our alternative to Bertolt Brecht's *The Good Woman of Setzuan* or *Mother Courage and Her Children*, using many of Brecht's epic theater techniques to tell the story of America in the midst of a series of crises on the eve of the millennium. Joan Didion will report to us in her distinctive new journalism style what was happening both to her and to America in the 1960s, particularly in the Haight-Ashbury district of San Francisco on the eve of the Summer of Love in her *Slouching towards Bethlehem*. Her canonical counterpart will be Charles Dickens, who taught the world how to combine techniques of reporting and fiction in his famous *Sketches by "Boz."* In Lecture 7, Mikhail Bulgakov's *The Master and Margarita* will bring the devil to Moscow in the most severe period of the Stalinist era, when no one in Russia was supposed to believe anymore in either God or the devil. His great books counterpoint, which he cites frequently in his novel, is Johann Wolfgang von Goethe's magnificent *Faust*.

The last five lectures will deal not with alternatives to canonical giants but with genres that are not (yet) considered quite canonical. This part of the course begins with Markus Zusak's *The Book Thief*, a young reader's book that tells the story of the "other" Germans in World War II—those who did not join the Nazi Party, who did not join the Hitler Youth Corps, and who risked their lives shielding Jews from Nazi persecution—through a fictional account of a young girl growing up on Himmel Street in the town of Molching, learning along the way the values of words and books in a world overrun by Nazi propaganda. Lecture 9, which focuses on P. D. James's *Death of an Expert Witness*, deals with crime fiction in the work of James, who inherited the genre from a generation of women writers and then expanded it by making characterization as important a part of crime fiction as it is in the mainstream novel. Character drives the plot in her books—rather than plot driving character—as was true of most of the works in the golden age of detective novels. Lecture 10 brings us to John le Carré's *The Spy Who Came In from the Cold*, a book published at the height of the James Bond mania that made the genre of the spy novel into one for grownups, focusing on the moral questions that beset a democratic society fighting an espionage war with countries of very different values and trying to decide how far one could adopt their methods and still be a culture worth fighting for. Lecture 11 features the newest of the literary genres, the graphic novel, which is really a comic book for adults. In Alan Moore and Dave Gibbons's *Watchmen*, a slightly parallel (to our) New York of 1985 confronts the terms of the cold war—the prospect of a nuclear holocaust—and treats these issues by putting into them a collection of costumed heroes and superheroes from comic books, who are all flawed in some way but who try to discover the identities of those who want to end life on the planet in order to prevent its demise. The final lecture addresses a best-selling blockbuster, Yann Martel's *Life of Pi*, which brings together many of the themes of the entire course, including the most important one: the significance and necessity of storytelling in our lives.

At the very end, the course reminds us again of the ways in which we can evade the pressures of someone's literary canon by finding books that can bring us the same satisfactions without the accompanying guilt and by assuring us that the world is full of great books that, while not canonical (at least not yet), can still bring us the pleasures and wisdom that literature can and often does deliver. We are invited to a lifetime of great reading!

A Skeptic's Way; Gogol's *Dead Souls*
Lecture 1

One of the best reasons for reading great books is that they allow us to establish personal relationships with them. We often use the great books, or the canon of great literature, as a benchmark, but the purpose of this course is to suggest books other than the classics that have the same effect. For example, Nikolay Gogol's *Dead Souls* provides a fascinating and interesting guide to Russia in the 1830s that is smaller in scope than Tolstoy's *War and Peace* but that still presents itself as a hybrid between an epic poem and a novel.

- The very term "great books" gives many people a shudder of apprehension. The great books are those that we know we should have read at some point, and the ones on the list that we haven't read we feel, in a slightly guilty way, that we *should* read—and probably the sooner the better.

- Enough people have told us that these books are good for us; that cultivated, intelligent people have all read them; that they're iconic; that we won't be able to understand our own culture or the world we live in if we haven't come to terms with them; and that we can't help but feel guilty that we haven't gotten around to them yet.

- The main purpose of this course is to analyze the idea that many of the same pleasures, satisfactions, and insights achieved in reading the great books can be achieved with other works—works that haven't been blessed with full canonical status.

- All of the works discussed in this course are great reads—a virtue they share with canonical works. Most of them, however, are shorter, more humorous, or less dependent upon allusions to other literature or classical references, or make less use of esoteric knowledge or difficult language—making them a bit more accessible so that they can connect with us, or we with them, without quite so many layers of resistance to work through.

- Along the way, we will define some elements that constitute a great read: For example, a great book can be reread with pleasure.

- Nikolay Gogol's *Dead Souls* was published in 1842, and like such works as Geoffrey Chaucer's *Canterbury Tales* or F. Scott Fitzgerald's *The Last Tycoon*, it's technically a fragment. While working on it, Gogol always talked about it as a three-volume work; fortunately, the first part is self-contained enough to stand alone.

- In his letters and essays, Gogol wrote that he admired a genre he called a minor epic, which included, on his list, Ludovico Ariosto's *Orlando Furioso* and Miguel de Cervantes's *Don Quixote*. The genre falls, according to Gogol, about halfway between an epic poem and a novel by taking a relatively insignificant character through a series of adventures that can give a lively picture of an entire age.

- On the title page of *Dead Souls*, Gogol called the work a ***poema***, which makes it an example of this hybrid genre that allows a writer to include a lot of material that would be difficult to fit into a conventional novel—and to include lyrical passages and digressions more appropriate to poetry than to prose fiction.

- In an interesting way, this idea of genre allows *Dead Souls* to share some features with one of its giant canonical counterparts: Tolstoy's *War and Peace*.

- Tolstoy started *War and Peace* as a society novel and opens it with a party that brings together a lot of his characters in one place, but then it becomes a family saga, a historical chronicle, a political novel, and finally a national epic—which is approximately where Gogol's novel ends up, too.

- Gogol's *Dead Souls* begins with the arrival of a stranger in a provincial town—and with a party that brings together many of its characters—and then moves out into wider circles until it becomes a novel about "all Russia," a national epic different from Tolstoy's (and with fewer pages and characters).

- The basic plot of Gogol's book involves the idea of dead souls, which was theoretically possible in Russia in the 1830s. Landowners had to report the number of serfs they had every five years and pay taxes on that number. If before the next census a serf died, the landowner still had to continue paying taxes until the next census, which was when he could report the death.

- If someone were to buy these dead souls cheaply, the landowner could stop paying taxes. Meanwhile, because the serfs were still legally alive, the purchaser could mortgage them at the going rate and acquire a lot of money in a short amount of time.

- As far as we can tell, Chichikov, the protagonist of Gogol's book, plans to use the money to buy himself an estate in order to become a landowner himself. We don't discover what Chichikov is actually doing until the last chapter; in his travels, his strange requests and behaviors puzzle the reader as well as characters in the book.

- The theme of the book is that the world is in a bad way—it has taken a wrong turn somewhere and fallen on evil times. It is an exposé of mortified, dead souls and creates a picture of the purposeless, senseless, sometimes ludicrous lives of Russians (and, by implication, all of mankind).

- The book is funny, often hilariously so, but the picture is bleak: Dead souls of title aren't just the serfs purchased by Chichikov—they are living characters, too, drifting aimlessly without any real sense of purpose or direction—beyond that of acquisition.

- Chichikov, who drives the entire plot, is in some ways deadest of all—motivated entirely by desire to acquire an estate and live the way other landowners do: He wants wealth, a wife and children, and then he can vegetate along with everyone else of his rank and class. It would take too long to accomplish these goals honestly, so he comes up with a scam that structures the book.

- In the last chapter, we discover that Chichikov's father provided a model of dishonest greed; from childhood, Chichikov has just wanted to be rich and comfortable—and that's who and what he is. Otherwise, he is a complete nonentity—neither handsome nor ugly, neither fat nor thin, neither old nor young—a perfect mediocre hero.

- What saves Gogol's book from bleakness of vision is its narrator—who is always present and takes us from place to place, explaining what we're reading about—and the devices and techniques he uses to give us a picture of "all Russia."

- Because Gogol saw this not as a novel but as a "minor epic," he included lots of material that was not strictly germane to his plot or appropriate for a novel; he does this with multiple digressions, lyrical passages, and some amazing **Homeric** or **epic similes**.

- In an epic simile, the comparison is extensively developed so that the secondary object (the one being compared to) becomes of interest in its own right—so much so that we sometimes lose sight of the primary object as the narrator gets carried away by the pleasure of his or her own comparison.

- Gogol's *Dead Souls* is supposedly about "all Russia," but it mostly deals with landowners and a few serfs—and most of the latter are treated satirically—so the plot actually deals with a very thin slice of "all Russia." Therefore, Gogol uses epic similes to bring in a mass of material about other aspects of Russian life.

Important Terms

epic (or **Homeric**) **simile**: An elaborated and intensified comparison in which the secondary object (or vehicle) is developed in such detail that it becomes interesting in its own right, sometimes leading a reader temporarily to forget the primary object (or tenor) that is being compared.

poema: As the term is used by Gogol, it refers to a genre that falls halfway between an epic poem and a novel. He cites Cervantes's *Don Quixote* as an example, and it is what he called his own *Dead Souls*.

Suggested Reading

Gibian, *Nikolai Gogol*.

Gogol, *Dead Souls*.

Setchkarev, *Gogol*.

Questions to Consider

1. In chapter 4, the landowner that Chichikov encounters is Nozdryov. What type of character is Nozdryov? What are his most striking attributes? What is ironic about his assumption that he and Chichikov are alike and that, therefore, they understand each other perfectly? What is the importance for his character of the many references to dogs, horses, and hunting throughout the chapter?

2. Chapter 9 features a conversation between two agreeable ladies discussing the affairs of Chichikov. Trace the steps by which the narrator describes how the merest speculation becomes established fact to be spread about the town in this marvelous satire on gossip in a provincial center. What kind of equivalent story do the men come up with? Notice, also, the epic simile of the sleeping schoolboy into whose nostrils his comrades shove a little bag of snuff as a way of describing how the town receives all of this news.

Orwell's *Down and Out in Paris and London*
Lecture 2

George Orwell provides an account of the underside of life in the Roaring Twenties in his novel *Down and Out in Paris and London*. Initially, the book appears to be a memoir in which an anonymous narrator reports on being poor in Paris and London. The book seems to be an authentic experience, but—although he does not alter or exclude facts—Orwell does rearrange some facts. The question to consider is whether "essentially true" is good enough.

- *Down and Out in Paris and London* is a story about a man (whom we take to be the writer, George Orwell) living modestly in Paris. He becomes ill and ends up in a public hospital (an experience almost as harrowing as the illness itself). Eventually, he gets better but then has the last of his money stolen. Forced to look for work but needing money even to look for a job, he pawns his good clothes and begins to discover what poverty is really like.

- At his most desperate, the narrator remembers his old friend Boris (a Russian refugee)—a waiter who has promised to help. After all kinds of adventures, none of which help the two men economically, Boris gets a job in a Paris hotel (which the narrator calls Hotel X) and gets the narrator a job as a *plongeur* (dishwasher).

- Eventually, a new restaurant opens, and both the narrator and Boris quit their jobs to work there. The restaurant is luxurious and elegant for patrons but is so badly managed and so filthy in the kitchen that the narrator quits in disgust.

- The narrator then writes to a friend in London, who has promised him a job. This is the transition from Paris to London. The job in London won't materialize for weeks or even months, so the narrator takes to the road, learning about life as a tramp or beggar, sleeping in casual wards attached to work houses, and taking charity from churches and the Salvation Army.

- At the end of each section, the writer steps out of his role as a narrator to comment on some of the injustices the poor face in France and England.

- As noted, this book seems like a memoir of actual experience, but from biographies and things Orwell wrote and said after writing the book, it is apparent that the material was rearranged—manipulated in ways that are more literary than journalistic.

- Orwell went to Paris not to study poverty but to write, he did so for a year, and then he got sick. When most of his remaining money was stolen, he had to scramble, spending as little as possible on food and shelter, pawning clothes, taking menial jobs, and ending up washing dishes at Hotel X.

- Orwell eventually accepted the failure of the plan and returned home to tutor a mentally impaired boy. It took him three years to work his Paris experience into the book; he rejected it at first because it was too short, so he then added the London section about tramping, which had been done *before* going to Paris.

- There has been a lot of attention to this kind of question over the years: Is this book a memoir, a sociological tract, a piece of journalism, a work of fiction—or some combination of these?

- Averil Gardner, in his book on Orwell, suggests that we can think of the book as a documentary, whose interest shifts back and forth between the recorder of the experience and the experience he records and between the personality of the writer and the reality he describes.

- All of this makes the book sound grim and depressing, but what keeps it from being so is its style and the narrator who comes to us through its style—who is very different from the flashy, digressive, nostalgia-loving, witty, ironic narrator we met in Gogol's *Dead Souls*. In Orwell's book, the narrator seems to almost disappear into the account he's offering.

- There is not much plot found in the story; rather, there is a series of vignettes strung along by the experience of the narrator, who supplies the eyes and ears so that we can take in the scene ourselves—with just the right details for us to remember them.

- To demonstrate Orwell's expertise, about 30 years prior to the publishing of *Down and Out in Paris and London*, Jack London spent time in London's East End and wrote *The People of the Abyss* (1903), noticing many of the same things as Orwell did.

- However, Jack London's style is very self-centered, melodramatic, and impressionistic. His sensibility is the center of all observations, and his prose is full of similes and dramatic subjective responses.

- Orwell, on the other hand, observing many of same occurrences, never allows his imagination to function in this way—a skill of documentary writers. Rather, he tries to produce responses in the reader as opposed to describing his own. Likewise, his prose is straightforward, subdued, and underplayed.

- Another virtue of Orwell's style is that it allows him to sneak in some subjective judgments without calling too much attention to them or causing us to want to challenge him.

- This is an important skill for a documentary writer: to make his observations sound so consistently factual that even when he slips in a judgment, we scarcely notice it. Everything is treated in a uniform way—the shocking or the sensational, the trivial or the questionable—so that the occasional judgment slips by us mostly unnoticed.

- Another feature of the book is its interesting gallery of characters, including Boris the Russian refugee, Charlie the runaway from a wealthy family, Paddy the Irish tramp, and Bozo the London street artist. As with everything else in the book, the portraits are created with a telling eye for just the right detail.

- The book is divided into two unequal parts (the Paris part is about 50 pages longer than the London part), and the tone changes when we cross the Channel back to London.

- The Paris part has some of the most cheerful prose Orwell ever wrote, despite the nature of the story. The London part is darker and less cheerful. Paris seems like a party, despite the poverty. At home in London, Orwell seems to have felt more responsible for the way things are, and the tone is more somber.

George Orwell did not go to Paris to study poverty, but once there he ended up living in a slum and washing dishes at a hotel.

- Furthermore, what charity there is in London is provided by churches and the Salvation Army, and both extract a high price for their gifts. In fact, the narrator comes to loathe Salvation Army centers; he says that they're so in the habit of thinking of themselves as a charitable body that they can't run a lodging house without making it stink of charity.

- We return to the initial question: memoir, journalistic account, or novel? How much can we fiddle with data and still call what we're doing a report? To what extent is "truth" compromised when it's delivered using literary techniques?

- Marc Weingarten, in *The Gang That Wouldn't Write Straight*, argues that writers such as Tom Wolfe, Hunter Thompson, Truman Capote, Norman Mailer, and Joan Didion changed journalism by incorporating into it devices usually reserved for fiction—called **new journalism**.

- One of the important precursors of these writers, Weingarten says, was Jonathan Swift, a solidly canonical writer who, in 1729, published "A Modest Proposal," which reported on the abuses of the English policy toward Ireland. Instead of reporting, however, he wrote a savage satire suggesting that the ultimate solution to the Irish problem was to have English people eat Irish babies.

- For Weingarten, Orwell is another precursor of the new journalists—in his case, using the techniques of a fiction writer to report the grinding relentless nature of menial labor, poverty, and the difficult task of staying alive for people living on the street.

- We know that some events in the book were rearranged and that some characters were composites—some events may even have been made up—but Orwell was just telling small lies in order to tell big truths, which would become a feature of new journalism 30 years later.

Important Term

new journalism: A school of journalism in the 1960s and 1970s that featured the use of literary techniques and devices in reporting. Tom Wolfe was its primary spokesman, and Truman Capote's *In Cold Blood* was one of its most famous achievements. Its most radical version was called gonzo journalism, in which the reporter participates so deeply in what he or she is reporting that he or she becomes the central figure of the piece. A notable example is Hunter Thompson's *Hell's Angels*.

Suggested Reading

Gardner, *George Orwell*.

Hammond, *A George Orwell Companion*.

Orwell, *Down and Out in Paris and London*.

Weingarten, *The Gang That Wouldn't Write Straight*.

Questions to Consider

1. Pawnshops are featured largely in Orwell's narrative, especially in Paris. What kinds of protocol are involved in visiting pawnshops? How do they reveal, in telling ways, what it feels like to be down and out? A famous incident in the book concerns a young girl who cuts off slightly more bread than the narrator has money to pay for. What does he do? Again, how do little moments like this shed light on the plight of being poor?

2. What do you think about the argument that the material in a report or memoir can be manipulated in order to present a larger truth? Does a failure to observe scrupulous fidelity of detail damage or even invalidate that larger truth? We all probably do something of the same when we tell stories about our own lives; if so, does that make the practice more forgivable when it occurs in print? Or does journalism need to obey a higher law than we do in the stories we tell about ourselves?

Cisneros's *The House on Mango Street*
Lecture 3

In *The House on Mango Street*, Sandra Cisneros records her life on Mango Street—even though she spends most of the book wanting to get away from there and wanting to be the kind of woman she sees in movies. In the end, she does escape: She will never be one of those tame women who spend their days waiting for their prince to take them away, but neither will she be someone who abandons her family and home, which compel her to write the stories of those who can't escape the confines of their culture.

- We ended our last lecture by raising a question about the relationship between fact and fiction—or between reporting and creating—that has teased critics and readers about George Orwell's *Down and Out in Paris and London* ever since its publication. We can ask the same question about Sandra Cisneros's *The House on Mango Street*.

- We know that the book is based on Cisneros's own experience growing up in an ethnic neighborhood in Chicago in the late 1950s and 1960s, but we might wonder to what extent she has rearranged the material to make it into the narrative she wrote.

- As it turned out, Cisneros revealed in an interview that she's writing *stories*—not an autobiography. As she put it, the stories she writes about are stories that she has either lived, witnessed, or were told to her—she just arranged them in an order that would make them clear and cohesive.

- Generically, *The House on Mango Street* is a collection of 44 short stories that can stand alone, but when read together in sequence, each acquires additional meaning in relation to the others. A canonical parallel to this kind of work could be Sherwood Anderson's *Winesburg, Ohio*, which works in the same ways.

- As in Anderson's book, some of the pieces in Cisneros's aren't fully developed short stories but rather sketches, vignettes, or prose poems, each of which is important in the overall shape and emerging themes of the entire work.

- The themes in *The House on Mango Street* are articulated in individual stories, and one of the largest themes is the subject of growing up female in what many Chicano and Chicana writers refer to as "the border"—that is, belonging in some ways to two different cultures without being perfectly assimilated into either.

- This is precisely the circumstance of Esperanza, the girl whose consciousness is the center of the book and who grows up during the course of the stories. There are enormous pressures on a girl growing up in a culture like that of Mango Street to internalize that culture's vision of women, which is almost exclusively confined to the roles of wife and mother.

- To live entirely within these cultural expectations requires making oneself attractive and alluring to men; Esperanza and her friends inadvertently do that in a story called "The Family of Little Feet," in which a woman in the neighborhood gives them a bag of old high-heeled shoes, which they wear up and down the streets. As a result, the sexual attention they attract from men is initially gratifying for the girls but is ultimately dangerous and frightening.

- Older girls in the neighborhood model this kind of behavior for Esperanza in ways that make it seem initially attractive and desirable. Almost everyone wants to leave Mango Street, but most of the young women who live there have so internalized the visions of their culture that they can picture themselves only as wives and mothers; their goal is to grow up quickly, get married, and get out.

- This paradigm is a dead end that is richly illustrated by many of the book's stories and vignettes. There are no happy endings for most of the women in the neighborhood, who have, in one way or another, escaped home only via marriage and motherhood. Since their roles involve turning themselves into sexual objects, what initially seems desirable—male attention and a validation of women—is simple reification, and we are presented with scene after scene of unhappy women.

- The stories of the various women who live on Mango Street—including Rosa Vargas, Mamacita, Rafaela, Minerva—are all softened in the telling by the fact that we're getting these stories from a young girl who doesn't always completely understand what's happening. Even so, these all turn out to be decidedly negative role models for Esperanza.

- The most compelling examples of this theme occur in a series of stories about a girl named Sally, who is a few years older than Esperanza and is admired by many of the boys at school. Esperanza's own sexual initiation occurs in two stories involving Sally: "The Monkey Garden" and "Red Clowns."

- What Esperanza believes is that there's been a vast conspiracy—of Sally, of other women, of books and movies—in weaving fairy tales about the subject of sex. Esperanza has been manipulated into a whole framework of cultural myths that become demolished in a way that allows us to see how her entire culture has made her vulnerable to sexual aggression and domination.

- Fortunately for Esperanza, there are some positive role models in her world, too. Her mother is a wonderful

Sandra Cisneros's *The House on Mango Street* is based on Cisneros's own experience growing up as a female in an ethnic neighborhood in Chicago in the late 1950s and 1960s.

character who tells her in "A Smart Cookie" that she could have been somebody if she hadn't been ashamed of being poor and dropped out of school.

- Most of the positive models for Esperanza are connected in some way with pointing her toward the writing career indicated by *The House on Mango Street* itself; similarly, the real house on Mango Street that she loathes and the dream house she has created in her mind function in this growth toward becoming an artist. Therefore, this book is both Cisneros's return to Mango Street and to the house that is her identity.

- As many readers and critics have noticed, this book is both a **Bildungsroman** and a ***Künstlerroman***. Both are German terms to designate, first, a book about growing up and coming to maturity as a human being and, second, about growing up to be an artist.

- Both of these literary forms have traditionally been about male protagonists: Goethe's *Wilhelm Meister's Apprenticeship* is a good canonical example of the first, and James Joyce's *A Portrait of the Artist as a Young Man* is an example of the second.

- The Bildungsroman follows a fairly standard pattern: a boy leaves home, undergoes trials, meets adversaries, and is successful in some kind of heroic act. In the process, he discovers who he is, becomes a man, and then is ready to reintegrate with his world—on his terms. Usually, his youth is spent in some kind of rebellion against his society, but having won his battles, he's ready to be reintegrated into that society at a higher level, achieving a balance between individualism and communal life.

- The *Künstlerroman* works in much the same way, except that the goal isn't so much integration into a community as the achievement of the status of being an artist.

- A woman's Bildungsroman (Jane Austen's *Emma*, for example) is traditionally different because it's always been less individualistic than a male's. She may undergo trials, but the point for her is to learn how to behave *in* society and how to assume her expected position in it—traditionally, of wife and mother. The rebellion stage usually doesn't happen, or if it does, it's relatively innocuous so as not to prevent the culminating marriage.

- *The House on Mango Street* doesn't end with the protagonist finding the traditional happy ending as a wife, as Emma does, but instead ends with a departure that promises a return—a way of integrating individualism with community as a Bildungsroman ideally does.

Important Terms

Bildungsroman: A novel that features the development of a young person growing up.

Künstlerroman: A special form of the Bildungsroman that focuses on the development of an artist.

Suggested Reading

Cisneros, *The House on Mango Street.*

Eysturoy, *Daughters of Self-Creation.*

Gutiérrez-Jones, "Different Voices."

McCracken, "Sandra Cisneros' *The House on Mango Street.*"

Nagel, "Sandra Cisneros's *Cuentitos Latinos.*"

Questions to Consider

1. A very short piece in the book is called "Bums in the Attic." How does this piece capture Esperanza's commitment to community rather than to a more individualistic development? How does this reinforce all of

the ways she is reminded throughout the book that she will never leave Mango Street—that it will always be a part of her and she of it?

2. Just about the only bits of nature left in the barrio in which Esperanza grows up are the four trees she can see from her window, growing out of and in spite of the concrete. How many times in the stories does she use these trees as symbols or metaphors? In how many different ways are they used? How many different parts of her aspirations do they come to represent?

Warren's *All the King's Men*
Lecture 4

Robert Penn Warren's *All the King's Men* is a book based, to some extent, on the career of Huey Long in Louisiana, but it transforms historical data into art. On your great books list, you can substitute Warren's book for Conrad's *Lord Jim* and *The Heart of Darkness*: You'll get much of the same technical skill, some of the same ideas, and a setting—Louisiana in the 1930s—that is delivered in a racy, colloquial style that will keep you turning pages until you reach the end.

- *All the King's Men*, first published in 1946, is another maturation story—this time of a young man who comes of moral, if not chronological, age in the 1930s of Huey Long's Louisiana.

- Huey Long, who was governor of Louisiana from 1928 to 1932 and then a U.S. senator from 1932 until his assassination in 1935, is an important historical figure for this novel—despite the fact that he isn't mentioned once in it. His literary counterpart in Warren's book is Willie Stark, whose character and career are largely based on those of Long.

- Huey Long was born in northern Louisiana, was minimally educated, and made his living as a traveling salesman while—incredibly—finishing a three-year law degree from Tulane University in eight months, mostly by studying on his own.

- After a few setbacks that taught him some difficult lessons about the nature of politics, he built a powerful political machine that made him governor at age 35. He survived all kinds of political attacks, impeachment proceedings, and physical assaults until, in 1932, he was elected to the U.S. Senate.

- To this day, Huey Long is a difficult figure for historians and biographers to come to terms with: He built a system of highways, eliminated poll taxes, expanded hospital services, and supported public education—but all of this was achieved through an administration that was deeply involved in graft, corruption, coercion, and cynicism.

- By 1932, Long was essentially the dictator of Louisiana; early reviewers attacked Warren for not focusing on Long's fascist leanings in an age that produced Hitler and Mussolini. Huey Long was assassinated at the State Capitol Building in Baton Rouge in 1935 by a doctor whose motives were more personal than political.

- The parallels between Huey Long and Willie Stark are too close to be ignored, and beyond biographical correspondences, there are moral ones. Warren puts Stark in the same morally ambiguous situation that Long was in, which demands the worst of them in order to survive—to finish the work they started. However, this still isn't a fictional biography of Huey Long or even a book about Willie Stark.

- Everything we learn about Stark comes to us through the mind and perceptions of Jack Burden, the novel's narrator—a technique used frequently in fiction, particularly in modern fiction, in which one character's story is told by another character.

- The relationship between the narrator and the main character can either be that of a detached narrator, in which the narrator tells someone else's story from more or less an objective point of view, or it could be that of an engaged narrator—like Nick Carraway in Fitzgerald's *The Great Gatsby*—in which the narrator becomes so deeply involved in the story that it becomes his own story as well.

- Because Jack Burden tells his own story while he tells that of Willie Stark, Jack serves as an engaged narrator in *All the King's Men*. As readers, we begin by being interested in the narrative of Willie

Stark's rise to power and his assassination, but what we experience is the way it all happens inside Jack's head.

- Jack's is a very different narrative voice than we've seen in the books we've examined so far; he is a Southern man whose sensibility is deeply and completely Southern. Jack is a historian who drifted into journalism, and his early assignment is to write stories about a young politician named Willie Stark—who was, at the time, the county treasurer embroiled in a controversy over who should build a new school.

- After a series of events that he narrates, Jack ends up as an assistant to Willie when he becomes governor. Jack's job is to research, which mostly means digging up stuff from the past that Willie can use as blackmail in order to get people to withdraw opposition or to fall in line with his plans.

- The whole novel is structured around three research jobs: The first is Jack's aborted dissertation on a distant relative of his, Cass Mastern. The second is to find something nasty in the past of Judge Irwin—a father figure to Jack when he was growing up—to convince him to withdraw support for one of Willie's opponents. The third is the novel itself, which is a trip back in time to try to understand both Willie's story and his own.

- As Jack notes, his and Willie's stories are connected, and both intertwined with Jack's research jobs for Willie, especially the one concerning Judge Irwin.

- When we meet Jack—a bright, talented researcher who is rudderless, lost, and without direction or commitment to anything—he is alienated from the world and from himself. Amused and detached from the greed and ambition that surrounds Willie, Jack does his job in what he thinks is a perfectly objective way, finding facts and letting whatever results happen.

- The purpose of the theories that Jack proposes—the brass-bound idealist, the great twitch, and the big sleep—is to keep him detached, morally innocent, and uncommitted in a world that he can see has a lot of evil in it.

- Jack believes that what you don't know can't hurt you, what you do know isn't real, and if history is a series of mechanical twitches caused by nerves and blood, there is no responsibility for what happens. Therefore, as Willie's investigator, Jack does whatever Willie asks him to do, and there is no morality involved for him—he just obeys orders.

- Eventually, the collapse of values by which he's tried to live shocks Jack into a new understanding. The stages of his growth, in a general way, involve the understanding that digging up what he thought was dead sets in motion a series of events that have tragic consequences for everyone he loves.

- As a result, Jack has to learn to take responsibility for his father's suicide and the death of Willie Stark. He also rejects his own theories because he saw too many of his friends die—all of whom lived in agony of their own will. They made choices that contributed to their own fates.

- The odds and ends of Jack's own life and world, which he had worked to see as disparate and disconnected from each other, begin to shape themselves into patterns in his mind. He sees that his friends, too, had struggled toward understanding and, therefore, share with him the responsibility for all that happened.

- At the end of the novel, Jack reconciles with his mother, who he has despised as long as he can remember; is married to his childhood sweetheart, Anne Stanton; lives in the house of his biological father, Judge Irwin; and has invited to live with them the man he had always thought of as his father and felt contempt for. He is also finishing his book on Cass Mastern—itself a sign of moral growth.

- There are two canonical works by Joseph Conrad that shadow this one: *Lord Jim* and *The Heart of Darkness*.
  - Both of Conrad's works use the same narrative point of view—that of the engaged narrator—and in both, the narrator is Marlow, who tells the stories of Tuan Jim and Kurtz, respectively.
  - Conrad also uses the same kind of broken chronology Warren uses in this novel, jumping backward and forward in time so that the pieces come together only gradually, like a great jigsaw puzzle.

Suggested Reading

Bloom, *Robert Penn Warren's "All the King's Men."*

Bohner, *Robert Penn Warren.*

Chambers, *Twentieth Century Interpretations of "All the King's Men."*

Warren, *All the King's Men.*

Questions to Consider

1. Anne Stanton has many functions in the novel: giving Jack an image by which he lives, helping to thoroughly disturb his worldview when she becomes Willie Stark's mistress, and becoming a part of his reconciliation with himself and the world at the end. Chapter 7 contains two striking moments in Jack's recollections of Anne: the deep dive into the pool and Jack's refusal to make love to Anne the night of the storm when Jack's mother is gone. What is the importance for Jack of these two memories? What do they tell us about Jack?

2. Jack says that the terrible division of his age is that between fact and idea, and he also says that as a student of history he could see that Adam, the man of idea, and Willie, the man of fact, were doomed to destroy each other but also to yearn toward each other and try to become each other. How does this idea work itself out in the course of the novel, and to what extent by novel's end is Jack able to bridge the gap between them?

Kushner's *Angels in America*
Lecture 5

As skeptics of the great books, we should read Tony Kushner's *Angels in America* in place of Bertolt Brecht's *Mother Courage and Her Children* or *The Good Woman of Setzuan*. While Brecht's plays are wonderful on stage, they don't read as well as Kushner's does—which, even in text, is a marvelous piece. It deals with a period of recent American history in provocative and interesting ways, providing us with many of the same pleasures, satisfactions, and experiences that we can get from its canonical counterpart.

- Tony Kushner's *Angels in America* is the general title for the two plays that comprise it, *Millennium Approaches* and *Perestroika*. The two plays opened in various ways—in workshops or staged readings—in 1990 and 1991, respectively, and had their stage premiers shortly thereafter.

- The works from the canon that can be used for comparison are Bertolt Brecht's *Mother Courage* and *The Good Woman of Setzuan*. Brecht has been called the most influential figure in 20th-century theater, and his two plays together were a genuine theatrical phenomenon of the 1990s, simultaneously managing great popularity and critical acclaim.

- Drama, doesn't offer a clear narrative voice like the works we've previously discussed; rather, each character arrives on stage, says what's on his or her mind, and acts out what he or she needs to on the basis of character and situation.

- The meaning of the whole play is found in the accumulation of these individual scenes, confrontations, and conflicts, which add up to something like a theme but that require readers to do more of the work of piecing it all together into some coherent idea or significance.

- Like the plays of Chekhov—or, in a different way, Brecht—there is no single central character in Kushner's *Angels in America*. The subtitle of the work is *A Gay Fantasia on National Themes*, and it focuses on a group of characters whose lives intersect with each other.

- There are, however, two couples that come close to being the central thread on which the plays are strung. The first is a pair of gay lovers, Louis Ironson and Prior Walter. In the beginning of the first play, Prior tells Louis that he has AIDS. Louis is a Jewish intellectual liberal, but he discovers that he can't face the prospect of watching his partner slowly die, so he abandons him to face AIDS alone. By the second play, the two rebuild a friendship.

- The second couple that is fairly central to the plays is Joe and Harper Pitt, Mormon husband and wife living in New York. Joe is a closet

At the end of Kushner's second play, the four central characters are gathered around Central Park's Bethesda Fountain, constituting a symbolic new society made up of male, female, straight, gay, black, white, agnostic, Mormon, and Jew.

gay, which he's known about for years, but as a good Mormon, he's spent much of his energy trying to suppress his inclinations. In the second play, he comes out of the closet, has a brief relationship with Louis, and then makes one last effort to return to his wife.

- The two plays include many personal, domestic scenes, but it's also—as the subtitle states—about national themes. Furthermore, it is also about identity politics, which are political actions based not on ideological grounds but on membership in particular communities: blacks, Hispanics, feminists, Christians, or—in these plays—gays.

- The plays' treatment of national themes is condensed in Angel, who comes to tell Prior of his mission. Prior is frightened, wanting things to go back to the way they used to be, so in some ways Angel is called into existence by Prior's own need. As a result of these hallucinations, Prior also worries that he might be losing his mind.

- Part of Prior Walter's identity involves being a descendent from a very traditional family. This is important because, in the second play, he's asked by Angel to be the prophet for a very conservative—even reactionary—message. The message Angel gives to Prior to give to humans is to stop moving, mixing, intermarrying, and mingling. Put down roots, and stay put.

- Eventually, Prior rejects Angel's message and refuses to be a prophet, but Angel's message really defines some overarching question of the plays: Is change possible? Can individuals change? Can cultures change? Can we change socially and politically in ways that can save the world from the kind of disaster angels see as inevitable unless everything stops immediately?

- There are some immense personal changes that occur during the plays. Prior has to learn to think of himself as someone dying of AIDS who was abandoned by his partner—and then as a possible prophet. In addition, Hannah sells her house in Salt Lake City to move to New York. Joe and Louis move out of settled relationships into new ones, which fall apart, and both do some serious soul-searching.

- The two religions—Judaism and Mormonism—that provide the mythic bones for the plays provide a model for change: God commands Abraham to leave home and travel to a new land, and in the opening visions of the Book of Mormon, Lehi is commanded to separate himself from the corrupt Jews of Jerusalem and take his family into the wilderness.

- Change isn't easy, and in the plays, both religions—both of which were based on change—have built-in resistance to change. All this resistance to the pain of change is embodied in angels, who have decided that everything can be fixed only if they can get humans to stop moving and changing things, to hold on to older categories and assumptions and structures of power, and then make everything stand still.

- There is one large vision that can help us understand the plays: The characters in the plays that learn how to change themselves and hope to effect some change in the world all discover that change isn't the simple obliteration of an old self or the repression of some parts of oneself. Earlier selves aren't left behind; responsibilities and commitments remain as characters transform.

- Many voices in the plays address issues from all kinds of points of view—so who do we listen to? One thing is certain: We shouldn't listen to the angels, who want to make the world less messy by making everything stop, which would also strangle the heart by sending the world back to a less complicated time.

- The canonical shadow for this play could be several by Eugene O'Neill, George Bernard Shaw, or Tennessee Williams, to all of whom Kushner has been compared. Perhaps the closest canonical plays we're reading this one in lieu of are some of Bertolt Brecht's: either *Mother Courage and Her Children* or *The Good Woman of Setzuan.*

- Brecht invented what he called **epic theater**, a form of drama designed to use various devices of alienation in order to enhance a play's didactic power. Kushner's plays are epic in many of the ways Brecht's plays are.

- Like Brecht, Kushner historicizes the events of his play by treating the 1980s as though they were a historical period; instead of having a single central character, he shows the impact of the social, political, and economic circumstances on a group of individuals caught up in them. Also like Brecht, Kushner is trying to teach us something by challenging our conventional categories of race, gender, age, religion, and sexual orientation.

- Kushner's plays also use a lot of Brecht's alienation techniques, designed to distance us from the events on stage and to remind us that we're watching a play. The idea is that if we're reminded that we're watching a stage play, not a slice of life, we won't get so caught up in the action, sympathetically identifying with individual characters, that we stop thinking about the issues the play presents.

- Kushner's ending is also very Brechtian: It is most like the ending of *The Good Woman of Setzuan* in that it doesn't tell us how change can really happen or exactly how we can recreate communities or what the new world would actually look like. Rather, it gives us a glimpse of the possibilities and sends us home to work out the details for ourselves.

Important Term

epic theater: While not entirely created by Bertolt Brecht, the term has become associated with him. Epic plays combine narrative and dramatic action and use what Brecht called "alienation techniques" that distance an audience from what is happening on stage to keep them from too closely identifying with characters and action so that they can remain critically awake—able to think clearly about what they are seeing. Alienation techniques include the use of short scenes, placing placards and lantern slides on the stage to announce what is happening, the use of songs and other interruptions (e.g. having the house lights come up and a character step forward to address the audience directly), seating the orchestra on stage, having stage sets put up in full view, and allowing those sets to look deliberately stagey or theatrical. Kushner uses many of these techniques in his *Angels in America.*

Suggested Reading

Bloom, *Tony Kushner.*

Fisher, *The Theater of Tony Kushner.*

Geis and Kruger, *Approaching the Millennium.*

Kushner, *Angels in America. Part One: Millennium Approaches.*

———, *Angels in America. Part Two: Perestroika.*

Nielsen, *Tony Kushner's "Angels in America."*

Questions to Consider

1. One of the things that people have admired about epic theater is that even the most loathsome characters are treated with some sympathy. Roy Cohn is clearly in this category, and Kushner treats him in such a way that even though it is clear that he disapproves of everything that Cohn stands for, we still feel some sympathy for him—how does he accomplish this? What part does Belize play in this amelioration? What about Ethel Rosenberg?

2. Why is it important that the final scene of the second play takes place in the presence of an angel at the Bethesda Fountain? What does the angel embody—vis-à-vis Angel, who tried to make Prior a Prophet? Why the Bethesda Fountain? What historical site is that fountain named for? What does Louis explain about it in the last scene? How does that help us to understand the presence of the stone angel as the final scene in a play about angels in America?

Didion's *Slouching towards Bethlehem*
Lecture 6

Instead of reading Charles Dickens's *Sketches by "Boz"* about Victorian London, spend some time with Joan Didion's sketches of 1960s and 1970s California—and other places and people—by reading *Slouching towards Bethlehem*. As always in our skeptic's alternative reading list, the pleasures and rewards will be equivalent. Along with Tom Wolfe, spokesperson for new journalism, Didion believed that traditional realist novels had been abandoned by avant-garde writers, who were writing such self-referential novels that they didn't bother to notice what was happening in the world.

- New journalists took as their models such 18th–19th-century writers as Henry Fielding, Charles Dickens, and Honore Balzac, who recorded their experiences in realist fiction. While the modern novel was, according to new journalism spokesperson Tom Wolfe, abandoning this ground, it could be reoccupied by journalists, who could use the techniques of the realist novel and create a new genre that was halfway between fiction and journalism.

- Traditional journalists attacked the form as a bastard that tried to have it both ways: exploiting the factual authority of journalism while having the entertainment and atmospheric values of fiction. The new journalists didn't disagree with the analysis, only the evaluation. They saw this hybrid combination as one of its strengths because their work could read like fiction—absorbing the reader the way fiction can—while carrying the truth value of reported fact. George Orwell was important in this movement.

- Joan Didion's essays are essays in the classical sense of the term, as created by the 16th-century French writer Michel de Montaigne: They're personal explorations that manage at the same time to be about the world around her, and the two parts—personal experiences and reporting—are always woven closely together.

- Didion's essays, in one sense, grow out of personal dread, but that dread is posited on the events occurring in the world around her, which either cause that dread or at least parallel it. The act of writing becomes personal—an act of recovery or at least an attempt at self-preservation.

- Joan Didion's interpretation of new journalism is to take what she reports on personally to tell us how the events of the world impinge on her consciousness so that as the world falls apart, she does too. Almost every essay is half journalism and half autobiography.

- In *Slouching towards Bethlehem*, only one section that consists of 8 essays is called "Life Styles in the Golden Land," suggesting that they're about California in the 1960s. The other two sections, consisting of 12 essays, are called "Personals" and "Seven Places of the Mind," suggesting that they're as much about the author herself as they are about the way the world was coming apart in the 1960s.

- Didion's primary subject in her early novels as well as in her essays is the meaning of California. Three of the best essays in *Slouching towards Bethlehem* are "Notes from a Native Daughter," "Some Dreamers of the Golden Dream," and the title essay "Slouching towards Bethlehem."

Joan Didion wrote the essay "Slouching towards Bethlehem" after spending a long time in the Haight-Ashbury district of San Francisco just before the Summer of Love.

- "Notes from a Native Daughter" is about old California—or at least the Sacramento Valley—and its meaning, both in itself and as a metaphor for America in the 1960s. For Didion, it's partly also a myth that she may or may not be correctly remembering. This essay is about what happened to California after 1950. In its changes, Didion finds a parable of the American tendency to forget history and to believe that one can start over, from scratch, with a blank slate.

- The only constant from Didion's California—the Sacramento of her childhood and the one in which she lived in the 1960s—is the rate at which it disappears. At the heart of her vision of California is the **Donner-Reed Party**, a group traveling in a wagon train that was forced to resort to cannibalism during the horrible winter of 1846 in the Sierra Nevada.

- For Didion, the example of the Donner-Reed Party becomes the endemic flaw in the frontier dream, the legacy of which still lives in California—the dream of escaping history and the corresponding breakdown of the kinds of loyalty demanded by the "wagon-train morality."

- The elements of this essay are all part of Didion's mythic California, which she admits is probably more myth than fact. She ends the essay by suggesting that perhaps it hasn't been about Sacramento at all but about the things we lose and the promises we break as we grow older.

- The myth of California is also at the center of the first essay in the book, "Some Dreamers of the Golden Dream." This essay is about Lucille Miller, who was from a fundamentalist home in Winnepeg. On the evening of October 7, 1964, on her way home from a late-night grocery-store run, Lucille Miller's car caught on fire and burned to death her husband, Cork Miller, a dentist in San Bernardino.

- Didion begins the essay by describing some of the San Bernardino Valley, making it virtually a character in the narrative. Then, she tells what happened to Lucille Miller on that dreadful night and describes the funeral of Cork Miller.

- Like other new journalists, Didion uses the omniscient point of view—so it reads like a 19th-century novel—to incorporate into the essay her own values as skillfully as did George Orwell in his book. Although the essay is about Lucille Miller, it's also about Didion's perspective on the California dream. California, after all, was built on the betrayals of the Donner-Reed Party and the snake that will always be in the garden.

- The best-known essay in the book is the title essay, "Slouching towards Bethlehem," which was written by Didion after spending a long time in the **Haight-Ashbury** district of San Francisco just before the Summer of Love. As much as any other essay in the collection, the essay gives a sense of the way the old order broke up in the 1960s—the way historical coherence was lost and both Didion's private and public worlds collapsed into chaos.

- This essay is one of the most brilliant pieces of journalism to come out of the 1960s, and as always, it's an account of how the world came apart for Didion at about the same time it did for America. There are accounts of runaways living on handouts and organizing their lives around acid trips, searching for some kind of identity. Many of the individual scenes are striking in themselves, even if they have no real narrative connection to the one before or after.

- Didion's *Slouching towards Bethlehem* can be compared to Charles Dickens's canonical work *Sketches by "Boz."* Dickens started the work in 1836 when he was a parliamentary reporter for a newspaper. His editor suggested that he spend some time telling stories about the people who lived and worked on the London streets, so he began a series called "Street Sketches," which were so popular that he continued writing them under the pseudonym of Boz.

- In the process, Dickens created a series of portraits of ordinary working men and women: bank clerks, shopkeepers, bakers, market men, and laundresses. Like the work of new journalists over a century later, Dickens's sketches were halfway between fiction and journalism, using techniques he would later use as a novelist and dividing his interest equally between what he was describing and the sensibility of the observer.

- In *Slouching towards Bethlehem*, Didion manages the same union of reporting and fiction, of fact and creative writing, and of data and interpretation that Dickens used, but her material has a freshness about it. While Dickens was a master of the 19th-century sentence, Didion was a master of the 20th-century sentence. Her writing is so disciplined, chiseled, lean, and focused that every sentence bears study.

Important Terms

Donner-Reed Party: A group of American pioneers who, on their way to California, were beset by delays and divisions within the group. One party was trapped in the snow in the Sierra Nevada Mountains in the winter of 1846–1847 and resorted to cannibalism, eating those who died of illness or starvation.

Haight-Ashbury: A section in central San Francisco (near Golden Gate Park) that, in the mid-1960s, became a center for the hippie movement, culminating in 1967—the Summer of Love—when the district was overrun with young people, flowers, music, drugs, and all kinds of alternative lifestyles.

Suggested Reading

Didion, *Slouching towards Bethlehem*.

Felton, *The Critical Response to Joan Didion*.

Friedman, *Joan Didion*.

Weingarten, *The Gang That Wouldn't Write Straight.*

Winchell, *Joan Didion.*

Questions to Consider

1. One of the sweetest and gentlest of the essays in *Slouching towards Bethlehem* is "John Wayne: A Love Song." What values does Didion find the John Wayne movie persona embodying? Why do they appeal to her so much? How (if at all) are they related to her "wagon-train morality"? Why is the thought that Wayne has cancer so shocking?

2. Another interesting essay is about Howard Hughes: "7000 Romaine, Los Angeles 38." Didion couldn't have known how Hughes would end up or that too much privacy can be a bad thing. What she saw in him in the 1960s seemed to be one kind of index to the American dream and character, telling us a lot about ourselves. What values, precisely, does she find embodied in Mr. Hughes?

Bulgakov's *The Master and Margarita*
Lecture 7

The juxtaposition of Joan Didion's *Slouching toward Bethlehem* and Mikhail Bulgakov's *The Master and Margarita* is interesting in that both in some ways are about revolution: Didion describes one that happened in Haight-Ashbury in San Francisco, which was allowed to run its course and fizzle out on its own, and Bulgakov describes one that had to happen under horrifically repressive circumstances in Moscow and couldn't express itself for many years after the events themselves.

- For reasons that were all too familiar in Russia during the Stalin years, Mikhail Bulgakov's *The Master and Margarita* waited a long time to be published. It was written between 1928 and 1940 in some of the most repressive years of the Stalinist regime, during which Bulgakov was frequently in trouble with the literary establishment or even Stalin himself for not keeping to the standards of socialist realism and ideological purity demanded by leaders of the Soviet Union.

- The novel is rich in plot and is about, in a general way, the necessity for the spiritual in human life. This notion was especially relevant in a Moscow that was, under the direction of Marxist-Leninist ideology, attempting to eliminate religion completely and confine the human spirit within the boundaries of dialectical materialism.

- At the beginning of the novel, a poet named Ivan and Berlioz, the chairman of the board of the Moscow Literary Association and editor of its journal, meet at Patriarch's Ponds in Moscow. They discuss a poem written by the poet that is about Jesus. Berlioz comments that the poem is not antireligious enough.

- Berlioz believes that it paints a negative enough picture of Jesus, but it still implies that Jesus was a real person who actually lived, which is unacceptable because the official verdict is that the whole Gospel story is a myth.

- In the middle of this discussion, they are joined by an unusual-looking stranger, Woland, who enters their discussion but claims that Jesus actually did exist. Woland tells the story of Yeshua Hah-Notsri (what Jesus of Nazareth is called) on trial before Pontius Pilate for sedition and says he knows it's true because he was there when the trial took place. We later discover that Woland is the devil.

- There are four main plots, or strands, that run through the novel, and they are all brought together in the last chapters of the novel.

- The first plot describes a lot of what was going on in the city of Moscow in the 1920s and 1930s. Much of this is satirical, focusing on labyrinthine Soviet bureaucracy and the amount of corruption involved at all levels. Nothing works the way it's supposed to.

- The most pointed satire is on theatrical and literary worlds, which had caused Bulgakov so much grief.

- The vices of theater people aren't specified, but the idea seems to be that the kind of people who end up as theater administrators are by definition hypocritical, greedy, inefficient, and pompous; in other words, they deserve to be treated roughly—as they are.

Between 1928 and 1940, Mikhail Bulgakov (1891–1940) wrote and rewrote *The Master and Margarita* six times, destroying several versions himself, to appease the literary establishment of the Stalinist regime in Russia.

- Literary establishment is given much more specific and precise satire. Several scenes occur at Griboyedov House, the headquarters of what translators call **MASSOLIT**, or "mass of literature": a state-run bureau of officially sanctioned writers who adhere to party ideology and write "proper" or "correct" literature.

- The state of literature, according to this picture, is catastrophic—an indication of the nation's decline. Bulgakov calls what goes on at Griboyedov House "hell," and ironically, Satan's Ball is attended later and is a much more civilized and graceful event than what goes on at Griboyedov House.

- Through a series of events, we learn that eliminating one person or burning down headquarters can't cure what is wrong with literature in Russia. In a way, this is Soviet-style identity politics—the kind discussed in Kushner's plays—with the special interest being writers and the issue the state of literature in a repressive totalitarian state.

- The second strand is the intrusion of Woland and his associates into Moscow life, which creates a fantastic world in the form of a grotesque carnival that disrupts life for four days.

- The idea of devils representing human vices and failings is an old one, but part of Bulgakov's purpose in introducing devils into Moscow is to illuminate the kinds of failures found in Soviet Russia.

- Woland is no ordinary devil—the kind that leads men and women into temptation to snare them for their own kingdom. Instead, he is closer to the Old Testament idea of Satan, in which he is God's adversary who tries humans and ends up working with God rather than against him.

- This is the pattern of the novel, but Woland doesn't even will evil: He ends up punishing those guilty of greed, selfishness, or self-interest, but he doesn't tempt anyone into doing these things or even delight in the evil he finds, either.

- This is a **Gnostic** view that good and evil, or light and dark, are dependent upon each other. Hence, Woland is a positive force. He still retains some devilish trappings, but his function in the novel is positive; throughout the novel, he is a figure of majesty and wisdom.

- The third strand is the love plot involving the Master and Margarita, which occurs mostly in the second half of the book.

- The Master is the author of novel about the story of Yeshua and Pilate that's at the heart of *The Master and Margarita*. Margarita is a strong, courageous woman in the tradition of Russian literature in which the women are stronger than the men they love.

- This love plot causes the Jerusalem story of Yeshua and Pilate, the story of modern Moscow, the supernatural forces at work, and the love story of the Master and Margarita to converge into a single story.

- The fourth and final strand is the novel written by the Master, the novel of Yeshua and Pilate, which is a superb novel within a novel. In a political way, this strand presents a theme of the entire book: the confrontation between state control and a visionary individual, which plays across all four strands of the novel.

- The canonical shadow for this work is Goethe's *Faust*, which Bulgakov cites in the epigraph and refers to dozens of times in the novel itself. Woland's name is from *Faust* Part II, and individual scenes come from the German work—such as the first scene at Patriarch's Ponds.

- Critics haven't really agreed on the precise way Bulgakov uses Goethe's *Faust*. Goethe was a certifiable genius who spent much of his creative life working on *Faust*, and hundreds of very brilliant and dedicated scholars have spent their lives trying to comprehend all that happens in that masterpiece.

- *Faust* is a great and important read, and Bulgakov uses it loosely—more for suggestion than for specific allusions that need to be understood and require a certain interpretation. Bulgakov takes us on a similar trip to Goethe's, starting from a similar premise, in a book that is itself challenging and can offer a lot of the same excitement without demanding that we spend the rest of our lives trying to understand it.

- Goethe's *Faust* has so many dimensions that it can mean many things, but one of the statements it makes is that there is an importance—even a necessity—of the spiritual in our everyday world. We like to believe—and casually do—that there is no God. Woland wonders if there isn't a God, who runs our lives, and who manages the world?

- Ivan believes that man governs himself, but the whole book demonstrates the problems with this view. Humans aren't just mortal; they are unable to guarantee even their next day.

- At the end of the novel, the spiritual triumphs. It's not really a Christian worldview because Bulgakov stripped the story of Pilate and Yeshua of all Messianic and mythical trappings to make Yeshua (Jesus) an interesting, committed, and deeply spiritual human being.

Important Terms

Gnosticism: A system of mystical and philosophical doctrines, Greek and Oriental in origin, that was modified by Christianity and includes emphasis on secret knowledge. As used in this course, it involves the more Platonic idea that opposites are dependent upon each other, implying that good could not exist without evil.

MASSOLIT: The acronym used in translation for the state-supported and state-sanctioned literary establishment in the Soviet Union during the Stalinist era. Bulgakov is both attacking the quality of literature produced and the Soviet fondness for acronyms. This one means something like "mass of literature." The notes in the translation used suggest that another way of understanding it is to think of it as LOTSALIT.

Suggested Reading

Bulgakov, *The Master and Margarita.*

Curtis, *Bulgakov's Last Decade.*

Natov, *Mikhail Bulgakov.*

Weeks, *The Master and Margarita.*

Wright, *Mikhail Bulgakov.*

Questions to Consider

1. If, as some critics have suggested, Yeshua represents the spiritual in Jerusalem and Woland represents it in Moscow, that would make the Master and Pontius Pilate parallel in some ways as well. Are there correspondences between the two that help to illuminate both characters? What are those parallels? Or does this turn out to be a nonproductive analogy in terms of reading the novel?

2. In Chapter 23, "Satan's Grand Ball," Baron Maigel is killed, and his blood is caught in a goblet by Korovyov. The goblet is then handed to Woland, who drinks from it and passes it to Margarita with the order to drink it. She hesitates, but when she drinks from it, it is no longer blood but wine. What New Testament parallel does this event recall, and what are the implications of that parallel for understanding the role and function of Woland in the novel?

Zusak's *The Book Thief*
Lecture 8

This lecture marks the beginning of a shift in our study, which will now deal with genres that traditionally fall outside the rubrics of literary canons. Markus Zusak's *The Book Thief* is an honest story beautifully told from an unusual narrative point of view. It is a story that reminds us of the other side of the German World War II story, and it can convince us, as it does Death, that human beings are pretty remarkable—in both horrible and astounding ways.

- Markus Zusak's *The Book Thief* is set in the German village of Molching mostly between 1939 and 1942. Molching is a fictional place that is near the nonfictional Munich, the headquarters of the Nazi Party, and **Dachau**, the first of the many German concentration camps. The novel never actually gets inside of Dachau, but it casts its shadow over much of what occurs in Molching.

- The story is focused on a 10-year-old girl named Liesel Meminger who, at the outset in 1939, is being taken along with her younger brother by their mother to Molching, where the children are supposed to live with foster parents. On the way to Molching, Liesel's little brother dies and is buried at a cemetery, where an apprentice gravedigger drops a book, *The Gravedigger's Handbook*, and Liesel picks it up—her first act as the book thief.

- Liesel arrives in Molching and is taken in by her foster parents, Hans and Rosa Hubermann, an ordinary couple who live on Himmel Street, which in German means "Heaven Street." Liesel is sent to school, but she can't even read, so she's put into a class of students much younger than she is. At school, she meets Rudy Steiner, who will eventually become her best friend and her partner in thievery. Eventually, Hans uses *The Gravedigger's Handbook* to teach Liesel to read.

- Liesel's second book theft occurs when the entire population of Molching is basically forced to attend a book burning on the occasion of Hitler's birthday in 1940. Liesel can now read, so she finds the vision of all those books being burned a disturbing one. In that moment, she realizes that Hitler is responsible for her father's disappearance, her brother's death, and the loss of her mother, who has also since disappeared. Liesel manages to save one book, *The Shoulder Shrug*, from the pile.

- A German Jew had saved Hans's life in World War I, so Hans had promised to help his family whenever he could. The man's 22-year-old son, Max, is now on the run from the Nazis and needs a place to hide, so Hans offers the basement of his house. The Hubermanns take Max in, and he and Liesel soon become friends.

- The wife of the aggressively pro-Nazi mayor of the town, Ilsa Hermann, had seen Liesel steal the book from the book burning. Rosa has a laundry service, and Ilsa is one of her customers. Liesel delivers the laundry each week, and one day, Ilsa invites Liesel into her vast library and offers her a chance to read more books.

- When Ilsa stops using Rosa's laundry service, Liesel begins climbing into the house

In *The Book Thief*, learning to read is itself a kind of thievery in which Liesel, the main character, can steal words back from Hitler and use them to subvert the official ideology.

through a window and stealing books from this amazing library. Meanwhile, Max has written two books for Liesel, painting over pages of Hitler's *Mein Kampf* with Hans's white house paint and then writing his book over them. The bond between Liesel and the hidden Jew strengthens each day.

- In 1942, a group of Jews is marched, under guard, through Molching on the way to Dachau. Hans offers an elderly prisoner a piece of bread and is whipped by the Nazi guard. Hans becomes ridden with guilt because he knows that Max must now leave the shelter of their home because, as a result of his offering to the dying man, his house will be searched, and Hans will be punished by being conscripted into the army.

- Meanwhile, Rudy's father must make a deal with the Gestapo: Rudy can stay home, but his father is conscripted into the military. So, Hans and Rudy's father are gone, and the war is going badly. Allied air raids happen often, and the residents of Himmel Street gather in somebody's basement to wait them out. On those long nights, Liesel reads to the frightened people.

- In February of 1943, just after Liesel's 14th birthday, Hans comes home. In August of 1943, Liesel sees Max, who is now one of the Jewish prisoners being marched to Dachau, and she walks with him in his procession until the Nazi guards whip both Max and Liesel.

- Soon after this, Liesel stops stealing books from the mayor's wife's library, but one day the mayor's wife shows up at Liesel's doorstep and gives her a blank book. Liesel then starts writing every night in the same basement where Max had lived and had written his books. What she writes is the story of her life: Its title is *The Book Thief*.

- Liesel is still writing on the night when the alert sirens don't go off in time and Himmel Street is bombed. Everyone she loves is killed in the raid that night; she survives only because she's writing in the basement. In her despair, she throws away her book. She's taken in by the police, who don't know what to do with her, until the mayor's wife takes her in. Eventually, Rudy's father comes home and takes Liesel in, having her work in his tailor shop, after learning that his son died in the bombing.

- At the end of the book, we're given a brief look ahead to what happens to the survivors. We find out that at the end of a long life, Liesel dies in Australia. Max shows up one last time, having survived Dachau, to find Liesel at Alex Steiner's tailor shop. Then, we find out what happened to the book, *The Book Thief*, so that we can read it.

- It is important to note that the narrator of the book is Death. It's a logical choice for wartime, but what's really interesting is the way he's portrayed: not as the scary figure of our nightmares but as an overworked being who is interested in humans. Because of his views, he collects stories that show that humans have another side. This story, about Liesel and the people of Himmel Street, is one of those.

- At the end of the book, we discover that Death had retrieved the book Liesel discarded, which is why he can tell us so much about her. The last time he sees her is when he comes to take her soul, and he says that it's time he returned the book to her. She asks him whether he's read it, and he says that he has—many times.

- Death, it turns out, isn't quite omniscient, but he's close enough to it to be a good narrator of Liesel's story, having to be many places at once in wartime and, thus, being able to provide us with information from beyond Himmel Street—information that Liesel couldn't possibly know and that puts her story into a larger context.

- Another remarkable thing about this book is that it tells us the other side of the German story of World War II. It tells the story of the Germans who didn't join the Nazi Party and who risked their lives to hide Jews in their houses. Zusak has said that his parents—much like the Hubermanns—were some of the people who resisted, and part of what he wanted to do in this book was to tell their story.

- The final striking aspect of the book is the theme of words and books: Hans teaches Liesel to read, and as Liesel learns to read, she gains a sense of identity and a sense of power. In addition, she learns to read in the context of book burnings and censorship, so learning to read is itself a kind of thievery—stealing words back from Hitler and the Nazis and using them to subvert the official dogma and ideology.

Important Terms

Dachau: A city northwest of Munich, it was the site of the first concentration camp in Germany established in 1933. It included laboratories that conducted medical experiments on the inmates, and it became the model for all later camps. It is estimated that about 30,000 prisoners died at the camp before it was liberated in 1945.

Mein Kampf: A book written by Adolf Hitler that was published in two volumes in 1925 and 1926. Its title translates to something like "My Struggle," and it is a combination of Hitler's autobiography and an exposition of his political ideology. It became a kind of textbook for the Nazi agenda.

Suggested Reading

Herbert and Herbert, *Book Club in a Box*.

Zusak, *The Book Thief*.

Questions to Consider

1. The Hubermanns have two grown children of their own who enter at intervals into the life on Himmel Street. What is their function in the novel? How do they help to define Hans and Rosa? Liesel? What do they contribute to our understanding of the nature of ideology and subversion in the book?

2. What is Ilse Hermann's story? She sees Liesel stealing a book from the book burning, and as the wife of a pro-Nazi mayor, she might be expected to turn Liesel in. Why doesn't she? What is it that makes her

reach out to Liesel? Are there ways in which Liesel helps her? Is Ilse's story one that Death might use as a way of balancing his ledger sheet about human nature?

James's *Death of an Expert Witness*
Lecture 9

The genre of detective or crime fiction is a popular one, and P. D. James is one of the genre's best writers. In *Death of an Expert Witness*—and, similarly, in *Shroud for a Nightingale*—James expanded the scope and reach of the detective genre from the classic English mystery so that it offers many of the same pleasures and insights found in non-detective fiction with the added bonus of having a wonderful puzzle to solve at its center.

- The classic English mystery was created and popularized in the 1920s and 1930s by an all-star cast of writers, most of whom were women: Agatha Christie, Dorothy L. Sayers, Josephine Tey, Ngaio Marsh, and Margery Allingham.

- In its fully developed form, a detective mystery features a fairly rigorous combination of characters, setting, and events that are arranged in a fixed pattern. A group of people is assembled in an isolated place (traditionally an English country house), and one of their members is murdered. The local police are called in but are baffled by the case: There are either no clues at all or too many of them, and everyone in the house turns out to have had the means, motive, and opportunity to have committed the crime.

- Because, as it turns out, everyone has something to hide, nobody tells the truth. To the rescue comes an eccentric amateur investigator who looks at the evidence, interviews all the suspects, constructs a case, and then, in a final climactic scene, gathers the suspects together, reconstructs the crime, and names the murderer.

- Behind this formula lie two assumptions: The first is that the world is a knowable and essentially rational place where everything can be known and has a logical explanation that can be achieved with the right intelligence, and the second is that the universe is an orderly and good place that is temporarily and shockingly disrupted by a murder.

- The detective penetrates this disturbed world, identifies the outlaw, removes him or her from the scene, and everything goes back to where it was before all of this happened.

- One of the reasons that mystery fiction is usually so satisfying is that it assures us that the world is basically a good place, that when one of us falls from grace he or she will be removed from it, and that evil is only a temporary and curable aberration.

- In all of these classical mysteries, certain things have to be sacrificed to make way for the puzzle, or plot, which is the essential ingredient. Setting is merely a background for the events, and the characters tend to be stereotyped and two-dimensional, fitting into the slots they have to occupy to make the plot work.

- Victims are expendable and not very interesting, and their murders seem mostly bloodless. In addition, the detectives are clearly fictional, eccentric enough to be comic or entertaining without us having to take them seriously as real people.

- This was the genre P. D. James inherited from her predecessors, and her achievement is that she pushed the genre well beyond where she had found it, creating varied and interesting characters whose actions spring from believable motivations and who stay in character throughout—both as victims and as suspects. What this does is to lift some of the emphasis from the plot and to shift it toward the other elements of the story, achieving a balance that brings her work closer to that of mainstream popular fiction.

- Her victims are also truly dead, and they are frequently described in graphic enough detail that we have no doubt that death is something more than an interesting puzzle to be solved by a brilliant detective. All of these things bring her mystery fiction closer to what we think of as the realist or realistic novel than had been true of her predecessors: All of her characters seem to be real people put onto the page.

- Her innovations are many, but we can simplify a bit by thinking of them in several related categories. The first is the way she uses setting in her work. Like the writers of the classical detective novel, she prefers to work with closed communities that have a limited number of suspects who know each other very well—sometimes too well—and who thus provide the reader with enough possibilities to be interesting and to be able to spend some time exploring the relationships among them.

- In both *Death of an Expert Witness* and *Shroud for a Nightingale*, the setting is important—it is, in fact, crucial to understanding the characters that inhabit this space and, thus, contributes to the eruption that brings death.

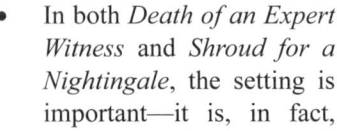

In detective or crime fiction, it is often an amateur investigator who looks at the evidence, interviews the suspects, constructs a case, and then gathers the suspects, reconstructs the crime, and names the murderer.

- Even more than setting, however, is the importance for James of the characters who live in these places. Adam Dalgliesh, James's detective, believes that the key to every crime is in the character of the victim, and he always spends time with the body before beginning his interviews. In the process of Dalgliesh's investigation, the first portrait that emerges from a James novel is that of the victim.

- By the time the novels are done, we understand the killers well enough to know that they aren't vicious or malignant or terrible people; instead, they are people who have been worked into a corner so dreadful that at some critical moment, the only way out they can see is to kill someone—which, of course, only makes their problems worse.

- The plot in James's novels grows out of character. Major characters get the most space, but every character gets James's full attention when he or she comes on stage, even if it's only for a page or two, so that long after we've finished one of her novels and have solved the puzzle, we remember its characters.

- But her most important characters, the ones that travel from novel to novel and hence get larger portions of her attention, are her detectives: Adam Dalgliesh and Cordelia Gray. Both of the novels we're analyzing feature Dalgliesh, who turns out to be the most fascinating of the many fascinating characters James has created.

- The other ways in which James has pushed the mystery genre into new territory involves her themes. The most important is probably the idea that murder is a contaminating event: The splash when you drop a rock into the water goes away—as does the investigation and the identification and punishment of the criminal—but the ripples go on and on, ending no one can say for sure where. Dalgliesh always knows this when he starts a case.

- In both novels, the investigation of the murder uncovers past mistakes, hidden fears, secrets, and personal longings. After each investigation, having watched what happens, Dalgliesh feels a great weariness. He knows that he can't do honest police work without inflicting pain, and the pain always reaches out in widening circles to include innocent people who just happened to get caught by the ripples.

- Another important theme is that of alienation—the feeling of being left out or out of touch with life. Everyone is alienated in James's books. Death is the ultimate indignity, and it alienates all of us. James reminds us in her books that we're all isolated and alienated by the disease of life to some degree. If that isolation is bad enough, it can be even worse than death.

- As critics have noted, James concentrates as much on the painful problems of being human as she does on the puzzle, which has broadened and deepened her mysteries until they become, in addition to good whodunits, good modern novels about us and our world as well.

- As we might expect, the endings of James's novels are not very joyous. At the end of every case, Dalgliesh has to feel that crime and guilt are everywhere—there is no single source—so redemption is impossible. The world is what it is, and nothing he can do will return the world to the pristine condition it was in before the polluting murder.

Suggested Reading

Gedez, *P. D. James.*

Hubly, "The Formula Challenged."

James, *Death of an Expert Witness.*

———, *Shroud for a Nightingale.*

Siebenheller, *P. D. James.*

Questions to Consider

1. There is a conventional way in which writers of detective fiction must "cheat" to avoid prematurely giving away the mystery puzzle. Because the point of view in this genre is almost always third-person omniscient, we customarily get to spend some time in the mind of the character who turns out in the end to be guilty; however, when we

are inside that person's mind and sharing his or her thoughts, he or she cannot think about the crime lest he or she give the game away, unnatural as it would be for someone who has committed a murder never to think about it. Does that kind of "cheating" occur in either of our two P. D. James novels?

2. P. D. James has stated that both she and her readers expect the guilty party to be caught and punished at the end of a crime novel, even if the writer has to arrange for the punishment himself or herself. A notorious example is what happens at the end of *Shroud for a Nightingale*, whose ending some readers have found unconvincing or even unbelievable. How does that ending strike you? Is it in character? Is it credible? Why do conventional forms of justice and punishment fail in this case?

Le Carré's *The Spy Who Came In from the Cold*
Lecture 10

John le Carré's *The Spy Who Came In from the Cold* did for the spy novel what P. D. James's *Death of an Expert Witness* did for the crime novel: It lifted spy novels out of the ranks of entertainment and put them into the category of books that can ask serious questions about us and about the relationship between the ideals that we profess and the methods we use to defend them—and the distance between them.

- In *The Spy Who Came In from the Cold*, John le Carré manages his expansion of the spy genre in a somewhat different way than P. D. James expanded the crime novel. In le Carré's book, characters are conceived primarily in terms of the roles they play in the plot. As critics have noted, le Carré's refusal to fill in backgrounds for his characters makes them seem less like social beings than agents of moral and political ideas.

- The book's central character is Alec Leamas, a British intelligence operative and a supposed defector. Liz is a British communist, an endangered species after the Soviet suppression of the Hungarian Revolt in 1956. Fiedler is a German Jew who has risen to prominence in the *Abteilung*, the East German Intelligence Service (another rarity, given the Holocaust). Mundt is a high-ranking East German intelligence officer with a Nazi background and, as it turns out, a traitor working for the British as a double agent.

- The central character is the spy who comes in from the cold, Alec Leamas, and one of the things that made this novel seem so new and interesting in 1963, when it was first published, was that it came out in the middle of the James Bond mania—and that Leamas is in almost every way a kind of anti-James Bond.

- Alec Leamas, in opposition to Bond, looks like he sort of drifted into the role of an operative at the Circus, headquarters of the English intelligence operation. He is anything but an intellectual, and he gets backed into corners by almost everyone he has conversations with. At the outset of the novel, he's just been recalled from Berlin to take on one more mission designed to get rid of Mundt, his antagonist from East Germany, in a most complicated setup.

- Leamas, again unlike Bond, is unreflective and not even particularly articulate. When pressed, he has a difficult time explaining why he does what he does and why he thinks that his side, England and the West, is worth the dirty games he's required to play for them.

- When Leamas is playing his role as defector and has been picked up by the East German *Abteilung*, he's interrogated by Fiedler, an extremely intelligent, articulate officer and a dedicated communist. Fiedler is primarily interested in finding out as much as he can from Leamas about the Circus personnel and operations, but along the way he's also interested in Leamas's philosophy—the ideas underpinning his actions.

- Fiedler, as a way of getting at Leamas's answers, explains his own creed, which he sees as the fight of socialism for peace and progress, in which the exploitation or even elimination of individuals can be justified by the collective good. That is, communism has a theory to explain why betrayal, treachery, and assassination are viable alternatives.

- On the other hand, Fiedler remarks that Leamas's society is based on Christian or at least humanitarian principles that assert the value of the individual. So, Fiedler asks Leamas how he justifies what he does. Leamas has no good answer, but he repeats an argument he's heard from his masters at the Circus: Even Christian societies have to protect themselves, and they can't afford to be any less ruthless than their enemies, even if their values are higher.

- This turns out to be a central issue of the book. Communist ideology always asserts the **utilitarian** principle of the greatest good for the greatest number and, hence, values the collective over the individual. Therefore, communist dogma can reconcile the loss of innocent lives with the progress of the proletarian revolution as necessary sacrifices.

- On the other hand, Western ideology values the individual over the collective and, therefore, should reject not only Soviet theory but practice as well. However, as Fiedler points out and as Leamas knows, the West quite frequently sacrifices the individual to defend the individual's right against the collective and, in the process, totally blurs goals and actions that should separate the two political systems.

- The novel stresses the ways in which—in terms of how they behave and what they're willing to do to fight the cold war—the two sides, as Fiedler points out to Leamas, are pretty much identical. In terms of the overall plot, there's a lot of material in the novel that supports this view. Toward the end of the novel, Leamas remarks that there isn't that much difference between East and West—between democracy and communism.

- The core of the novel is a series of confrontations between Leamas and someone who either tries to convince him of an ideology or who questions him about his. There are four such confrontations: the first with Control, the second with Liz, the third with Fiedler, and the final one with Liz again.

- In Leamas's final confrontation with Liz, he argues that, in a fallen world, to employ what is foul is acceptable if it's done to prevent something worse—in this case, World War III. Liz, the nominal communist, argues for the sanctity of the individual and condemns all actions based on expediency; she lives in a world of absolutes.

- As Liz walks toward the Berlin Wall in the final chapter, she walks stiffly: She's already dead, refusing any longer to live in a world that finds these kinds of rules acceptable. Alec decides the moment she is shot by the *Abteilung* that she's right, and he climbs down on the eastern side of the wall and waits until the *Abteilung* kill him, too.

- For some readers, Liz's vision is the meaning of the novel. Liz was caught between East and West and is therefore dead. She's been used in the most cynical and callous way in the name of higher ideals, and her murder was planned as part of the operation. The Circus is no more concerned for the individual than the East German communists are. Fiedler was right: Both sides are the same.

- How much does Leamas learn during the course of the novel? Leamas has many learning experiences, but the only lesson he appears to have learned at the end is that of nihilism: Nothing matters.

In the climactic moment of *The Spy Who Came In from the Cold*, Alec Leamas climbs down to the east side of the Berlin Wall and waits to be killed—an event that is interpreted differently by various critics.

- Still, he climbs back down to the east side of the wall and waits for the *Abteilung* to kill him, falling next to Liz. This, the climactic moment of the entire novel, has been read in several ways.

- For some, Leamas, aware of the moral vacuum at the center of world politics, chooses death with the one person he loves rather than live with what he knows, making his final gesture an act of defiance against both sides of the wall. For others, at the moment when he climbs back down the wall, Leamas abandons his own code to endorse Liz's.

- For still others, the ending is a kind of failure, allowing us an emotional response to the novel when the lovers die together, confused, without resolving any of the issues the novel has raised. For still others, Leamas's choice to climb down the wall to die with Liz restores the humanity he had to abdicate to serve the system, choosing love over his profession and individualism over institutional tyranny.

- The Berlin Wall is down, and the cold war is over—or at least the players have changed. However, the concern this novel raises is still important in our world: The only thing worth fighting for is the individual, and that's the one thing neither side any longer cares about.

Important Terms

Abteilung: During World War II, the German word that referred to a military formation, but later—in civilian usage—it came to mean something like "office department." It became the name for the East German Intelligence Service.

utilitarianism: A philosophy, associated primarily with Jeremy Bentham and John Stuart Mill, that argues that usefulness is the primary moral criterion of action and that the greatest extent of human happiness determines the highest moral good—in epigrammatic terms, "the greatest good for the greatest number of people."

Suggested Reading

Barley, *Taking Sides.*

Cobbs, *Understanding John le Carré.*

Homberger, *John le Carré.*

le Carré, *The Spy Who Came In from the Cold.*

Lewis, *John le Carré.*

Questions to Consider

1. As far as you can tell from the novel, what part does George Smiley play in the creation of the many-sided plot to discredit (and destroy) Fiedler and empower Mundt within the *Abteilung*? How often does he appear? What parts does he play? Do his disclaimers strike you, after reading the entire novel, as genuine? Or as yet another layer of deceit and subterfuge that marks the entire operation of the Circus?

2. In 1965 in England, class distinctions still meant a great deal, even though the lines between them were softening. Read carefully the interview, early in the novel, between Control and Leamas. How does Control exploit his class superiority to maneuver Leamas into a corner? What specific techniques does Control use to keep reminding Leamas that Control is from a different (and superior) class? Well trained as Leamas is in English class politics, how does he react to this manipulation? How do Leamas's responses in this crucial interview help to characterize him?

Moore and Gibbons's *Watchmen*
Lecture 11

The graphic novel genre is still, in most places, pretty far outside the traditional categories of canonical books. In a way, graphic novels—such as Alan Moore and Dave Gibbons's *Watchmen*—have allowed people who grew up with comic books to be able to continue their relationship with them without being embarrassed because a graphic novel is a serious art form that is capable of dealing with ideas as challenging as those in literature or film.

- Alan Moore and Dave Gibbons's *Watchmen* is a graphic novel, which is a book of sequential art (that is, comics) of any style that covers a broad range of subjects, including autobiography, journalism, biography, and history. It's also of considerable length, and it has to be read sequentially—not the way we might read a collection of comic strips.

- *Watchmen* deals with the costumed heroes and superheroes of our childhood—the sort of comic figures that were launched with the first *Superman* comic in 1938. However, Moore and Gibbons created a new set of comic book heroes—based roughly on heroes from DC Comics and Charlton Comics—that they could develop in whatever ways they chose, and they could be one-off characters because they wouldn't appear in a future series.

- Nite Owl has many of Batman's characteristics, including a fascination with gadgets and even a sort of Batcave in the basement of his house.

- The Comedian, who's killed in the first chapter but whose story is filled in by the remembrances of other characters in the following eleven chapters, is a kind of dark version of Captain America.

- Silk Spectre I and II, a mother and daughter from different generations of costumed heroes, are more or less Wonder Woman—even down to their costumes.

- Dr. Manhattan, who's been the victim of a nuclear accident, is a kind of mutation; he's the only hero with superpowers, and he's very loosely drawn along the same lines as Superman.

- Ozymandias is a self-made hero—brilliant, beautiful, and strong—who, in a kind of **Nietzschean superman** way, has developed his powers until he seems no longer quite human. He is roughly based on the DC Comics version of Marvelman, an adaptation of the earlier British Miracleman and other earlier costumed heroes.

- Rorschach, the vigilante who preys on the fears of criminals but who operates almost completely outside the bounds of the society he protects—and whose name comes from the shifting shapes on the mask he wears—is probably based on the Charlton hero The Question.

- Despite these characters' descent from earlier comic book heroes, Moore and Gibbons cast their characters in darker, more ordinarily human shades, undercutting in some ways their status as heroes and superheroes. They're all at least middle-aged, and they're all flawed in some way—the same ways, in fact, that other human beings are flawed. To make their situations even more interesting, Moore and Gibbons have placed them in a realistic world. It's not quite our world; it's one that exists parallel to ours.

- The year of the *Watchmen* story is 1985, but it's not quite our 1985—because of the characters that are central to this story. For example, the accidental creation of Dr. Manhattan in the nuclear accident tipped the balance of power in the cold war in favor of the United States because the Russians had nothing to counter him.

- In the graphic world of 1977, both the police and the general population became frustrated with the costumed heroes' interference in their work and lives; the police went on strike, causing Congress to pass a law against vigilantism. Most of the costumed heroes in the book have thus been retired for eight years.

- Otherwise, however, the America of 1985 seems familiar: The Soviets and Americans are in a deadly weapons race, each stockpiling nuclear warheads that could destroy the planet many times over. In fact, the presence of Dr. Manhattan on the American side has actually increased the tension; the reasoning is that the Russians might plan a preemptive strike to avoid being controlled by the United States.

- The main plot of the novel follows the consequences of the brutal murder of one of the costumed heroes: the Comedian. The murder awakens in Rorschach the suspicion that someone is trying to kill off the heroes, and the idea gains credence from several other events, including a smear campaign against Dr. Manhattan that sends him off the planet entirely—to Mars, to be precise.

- It begins to seem clear to the heroes working on the case that there's a conspiracy afoot to eliminate them, and especially Dr. Manhattan, so that the Soviets can be more aggressive, prompting America to retaliate and, thus, to precipitate in Armageddon.

- Who, the question is, could be behind such a plan? Who would want to destroy the world? That's only the question of the main plot. Most of the subplots involve ordinary people going about their lives in the growing fear of a war to end not just all wars but all human life on Earth. One of the real virtues of the book is the way many of the minor characters are developed and whose stories manage to get told in the shade of the larger plot.

- There is a graphic novel within a graphic novel—called "Marooned" from a series called *The Black Freighter*—that serves a variety of functions in *Watchmen*. It is so beautifully interleaved with our story that, quite often, remarks that we overhear from the news vendor while we're reading the comic book with the young boy serve to make commentary on the comic—and to allow the comic to make commentary on the New York plot.

- This kind of parallel structure works throughout the novel. There are multiple plots, and they are skillfully interleaved, drawing our attention to contrasts and parallels among them and allowing each plot to be a **foil** for the others.

- The design and the art of the book tie its many strands together. One of the book's unifying symbols is a smiley face, which appears on the cover of the first issue. It turns out to be a button the Comedian wore when he was thrown out of his high-rise apartment window, and when the body is taken away, the button remains in a pool of blood just beside a sewer grate. The button itself has one little drip of blood across its right eye, and this image shows up repeatedly in the book.

Dr. Manhattan, who has been the victim of a nuclear accident, is the only hero in *Watchmen* that has superpowers and can travel to the craters of Mars at a moment's notice.

- Another feature of this book is the intercalary material. Between each pair of chapters are four pages of essay or a collage of text material relating to the theme and background of that chapter or developing the storyline as a whole.

- These intercalary materials provide much of the texture for the book, providing information that makes the graphic pages themselves richer and more resonant. Some of these essays do a lot of the expository work for the novel, and they also deal with the issue of why someone chooses to become a masked hero and admit a variety of motives besides the need for justice—one of the motives for the first generation of costumed warriors.

- Critics have suggested that what Moore and Gibbons are asking in this book is how far we should trust our guardians, whether they're outlawed heroes coping with midlife crises or our own governments or superpowers bent on global war.

- Another way of thinking about the book—as suggested by Moore—is as a kind of warning to Americans about bullying. The point is that a society that thinks it can do anything because it's invulnerable can gloss over nuclear stockpiles and the world situation and think that it can do what it wants.

- The book asks, "Who watches the watchmen?" and there are no ultimate answers: They watch each other, they watch themselves, the rest of the world watches them, and we as readers watch them, too. The book reminds us that in many ways the entire history of superhero comics is loaded with questions about power and the way that power affects and changes us.

Important Terms

foil: Literally, a piece of metal placed under a jewel to set it off. In literature, it refers to a person or event that, via contrast, underscores the characteristics of another person or event. For example, Laertes and Fortinbras are both foils to Hamlet.

Nietzschean superman: A concept associated with German philosopher Friedrich Nietzsche (1844–1900), for whom the *Übermensch* was a hypothetical but possible future being characterized by physical perfection—a capacity for power and a moral nature beyond good and evil.

Rorschach test: An inkblot test developed by the Swiss psychologist Hermann Rorschach in which inkblots are perceived and interpreted by patients, and then their responses are analyzed to yield psychological insights. In *Watchmen*, the character known as Rorschach takes his name from the mask he wears, which resembles an inkblot whose pattern is always shifting.

Suggested Reading

Fingeroth, *The Rough Guide to Graphic Novels*.

Gravett, *Graphic Novels*.

Kaveney, *Superheroes!*

Moore and Gibbons, *Watchmen*.

Reynolds, *Super Heroes*.

Questions to Consider

1. Each chapter of *Watchmen* is titled, and the title comes from a quotation that ends the chapter. For example, chapter 1 is "At midnight, all the agents … "—a quotation from Bob Dylan's "Desolation Row." Other quotations come from Elvis Costello, the book of Genesis, Albert Einstein, William Blake, Friedrich Nietzsche, the book of Job, Eleanor Farjeon, Carl Jung, Percy Shelley, and John Cale. We've already suggested the way that the Nietzsche quotation in chapter 6 applies to Dr. Malcolm Long. What do you make of the relevance of the other quotations to their respective chapters?

2. It has been suggested that the first generation of costumed heroes (the Minutemen), especially as they are depicted in the excerpts from Hollis Mason's *Under the Hood* in the first three intercalary pieces, comes

from and represents a younger, happier, more innocent time in American history. Does that seem to be a valid assessment? If so, what factors account for the differences between the first and second generations of costumed heroes?

Skeptics and Tigers; Martel's *Life of Pi*
Lecture 12

In the last lecture of this course, the focus is on the final non-canonical genre: the blockbuster best seller. It's the kind of book that everyone seems to be talking about, and there is even talk of an impending motion picture. Yann Martel's *Life of Pi* is just such a book, and it can give—as all the books in this course have—the same pleasures, satisfactions, and stimulation we get from the great books.

- Yann Martel's *Life of Pi* is about a 16-year-old boy who grew up in Pondicherry in South India, where his father owned and managed a zoo. In the mid-1970s, Pi's father becomes disenchanted with the policies and practices of the Indian prime minister and decides to sell his zoo and move to Canada.

- It takes him a year to find new homes for all the animals except the ones traveling with the family to new homes in Canada, and the remaining animals and people travel on the same boat: the Japanese *Tsimtsum*. Along the way, the boat sinks, and by sheerest happenstance, Pi is the only human survivor. He ends up adrift in the Pacific on a lifeboat with a full-grown Bengal tiger, whose name at the zoo was Richard Parker.

- The story tells of a 227-day ordeal that requires Pi to use all the skills he learned at his father's zoo to dominate Richard Parker enough so that they can share the boat, while Pi learns how to catch enough sea turtles, fish, birds, and the occasional baby shark—and rainwater—to keep the two (just barely) alive.

- Eventually, they land on a Mexican beach, where Richard Parker runs off into the jungle without—to Pi's great distress—acknowledging Pi in any way. Pi is found and is taken to the hospital. After he is partly recovered, two Japanese inspectors come to inquire about the sinking of *Tsimtsum*.

- Pi tells the inspectors his story, which they refuse to believe, so he tells an alternate version—the same story but without any animals in it. In the end, Pi asks them which story they prefer, and the book ends with the report the inspectors prepare about their interview, which closes the case of the *Tsimtsum*.

- *Life of Pi* can be read in many ways, but it is most obviously a survival story. Much of the time, we're at sea learning how to use survival skills on a lifeboat.

- In Pi's case, however, the survival stakes are much higher because he has to tame a tiger that shares the space with him in order to keep him on one side of the boat. As a result, we learn a lot about human-animal relationships along the way.

- As we're reading, we realize that this book speaks to us on other levels as well. Clearly, it's a spiritual journey—a growing-up experience for Pi—and the kind of growth is very specific to this character, this set of events, and this place and time.

- Part I of the novel focuses on Pi's childhood, which is marked by (among other things) a deep thirst for spiritual knowledge. He is the child of secular parents who is taken to a Hindu temple by his aunt and immediately falls in love with Hinduism.

- Later, he discovers a Catholic church that fascinates him and meets a friendly priest who tells him about the suffering of Jesus who—even though he was God—did what he did out of love. Still later, Pi comes to a baker's shop just as the baker is kneeling on a Muslim prayer rug and becomes further intrigued.

- Pi is converted by both Catholic and Muslim faiths, but he doesn't substitute them for his Hinduism; instead, he adds them, so he's simultaneously a Hindu, Catholic, and Muslim. In a comic scene in Chapter 23 of Part I, Pi's priest, **imam** (Muslim leader), and **pandit** (Hindu scholar) all run into Pi at the same time and spend a lot of time arguing over him and over the relative merits of their religions.

- This union of three faiths works for Pi, and his life from then on is marked by some fantastic religious experiences. These religious resources help him a lot as he's crossing the Pacific in a lifeboat with a Bengal tiger—but they aren't his only resources because, thanks to his father and one of his teachers, he's also a scientist.

- Pi's favorite teacher at school is a biologist and atheist who believes in the power of science. Pi knows that it is science that teaches us how to survive in the world, but he still believes in science and God. What emerges for Pi out of this marriage of science and faith is that science can explain the world up to a certain point—and it's very good at what it does—but at that certain point that its usefulness ends, religion has to take over.

- The two characters, Pi and Richard Parker, occupy the two sides of the lifeboat in Part II in a very explicit way, making a kind of allegory of Pi's spiritual journey. In one half of the boat is Richard Parker, a pure and beautiful animal, and in the other half is a boy who is so religious that he believes in three faiths at once. Part of the purpose of the 227 days at sea is the reconciliation of the two halves that are found within Pi: science and faith.

In *Life of Pi*, a teenager named Pi is stranded for 227 days on a lifeboat with a Bengal tiger, which Pi must tame to keep the peace until they land on a beach in Mexico.

- For survival, Pi needs to be a scientist, an animal trainer; in some ways, he even has to become an animal himself to do what he has to do to survive another day. This part of him is dominant while on the lifeboat: He notices how, each day, he becomes more like Richard Parker. At the same time, even in the worst times, Pi tries to keep alive his religious sense of wonder of the world and the ways in which the divine can sometimes shine through the natural.

- There is a complicated point of view used in this story that illuminates these themes. It begins with a first-person narration about a novelist having trouble writing the next novel. Then, in a coffee shop in Pondicherry, the novelist meets an old man who says he knows a story that will make the novelist believe in God. This man sends the novelist to Canada, where he will find the Mr. Patel whose story this is.

- From this point forward, we expect a first-person detached story, in which the narrator tells someone else's story, or a third-person account. Instead, the novelist says that since it's Mr. Patel's story, it should be told in first person—as though Mr. Patel is telling it to us himself—so that's the way we read the story. The novelist breaks in several times to remind us that he's still there, mediating Pi's story to us. Pi's story ends when he and Richard Parker reach Mexico, and then the novelist takes over for the last seven chapters.

- In this way, as we're reading the book, we are given the same test the investigators are given: Which story do we prefer, and why do we choose as we do? Is it possible that we believe in God the way we believe in fiction because it makes a better story? And if so, is there anything wrong with that?

- In this course, we have been all over the place in terms of themes, subjects, styles, and genres—but there has been one common denominator: We think that all of the books we've encountered are worth the read. The world is full of books that, if we take the time to work with them, will yield as much satisfaction, pleasure, stimulation, and insight as some of their more prestigious counterparts.

- Our last book has reminded us that we do have choices to make both in what we read and how we read. We can have the story, our personal book list, and this course—as Pi would put it—with animals or without animals. Which do you prefer?

Important Terms

Atman: In Hinduism, the supreme soul and the divine soul in each human being; when capitalized, it is the source and goal of all individual souls.

imam: A Muslim leader who recites prayers and leads devotions.

pandit: In Hinduism, a scholar skilled in Sanskrit and Hindu law and religion.

Suggested Reading

Cullina, *ClassicNotes GradeSaver: "Life of Pi."*

Eagleton, *Literary Theory*.

Martell, *Life of Pi*.

Questions to Consider

1. Research online (or in some suitable printed source) the word "Pondicherry," the former capital of what was once French India. Why does it make such a great place for Pi to spend his early years, and what contribution might it have made to his conversion to three religions at one time?

2. Pi spends a lot of time in the first half of the novel defending zoos. How does he defend them, and against what kinds of attacks? How convincing do you find his defense? In what way (if at all) is a zoo a good place for a wild animal?

Glossary

Abteilung: During World War II, the German word that referred to a military formation, but later—in civilian usage—it came to mean something like "office department." It became the name for the East German Intelligence Service.

Bildungsroman: A novel that features the development of a young person growing up.

Dachau: A city northwest of Munich, it was the site of the first concentration camp in Germany established in 1933. It included laboratories that conducted medical experiments on the inmates, and it became the model for all later camps. It is estimated that about 30,000 prisoners died at the camp before it was liberated in 1945.

Donner-Reed Party: A group of American pioneers who, on their way to California, were beset by delays and divisions within the group. One party was trapped in the snow in the Sierra Nevada Mountains in the winter of 1846–1847 and resorted to cannibalism, eating those who died of illness or starvation.

epic (or **Homeric**) **simile**: An elaborate and intense comparison in which the secondary object (or vehicle) is developed in such detail that it becomes interesting in its own right, sometimes leading a reader temporarily to forget the primary object (or tenor) that is being compared.

epic theater: While not entirely created by Bertolt Brecht, the term has become associated with him. Epic plays combine narrative and dramatic action and use what Brecht called "alienation techniques" that distance an audience from what is happening on stage to keep them from too closely identifying with characters and action so that they can remain critically awake—able to think clearly about what they are seeing. Alienation techniques include the use of short scenes, placing placards and lantern slides on the stage to announce what is happening, the use of songs and other interruptions (e.g. having the house lights come up and a character step forward to address the audience directly), seating the orchestra on stage, having stage sets put up in full view, and allowing those sets to look deliberately stagey or theatrical. Kushner uses many of these techniques in *Angels in America.*

foil: Literally, a piece of metal placed under a jewel to set it off. In literature, it refers to a person or event that, via contrast, underscores the characteristics of another person or event. For example, Laertes and Fortinbras are both foils to Hamlet.

Gnosticism: A system of mystical and philosophical doctrines, Greek and Oriental in origin, that was modified by Christianity and includes emphasis on secret knowledge. As used in this course, it involves the more Platonic idea that opposites are dependent upon each other, implying that good could not exist without evil.

Haight-Ashbury: A section in central San Francisco (near Golden Gate Park) that, in the mid-1960s, became a center for the hippie movement, culminating in 1967—the "Summer of Love"—when the district was overrun with young people, flowers, music, drugs, and all kinds of alternative lifestyles.

imam: A Muslim leader who recites prayers and leads devotions.

Künstlerroman: A special form of the Bildungsroman that focuses on the development of an artist.

MASSOLIT: The acronym used in translation for the state-supported and state-sanctioned literary establishment in the Soviet Union during the Stalinist era. Bulgakov is both attacking the quality of literature produced and the Soviet fondness for acronyms. This one means something like "mass of literature." The notes in the translation used suggest that another way of understanding it is to think of it as LOTSALIT.

Mein Kampf: A book written by Adolf Hitler that was published in two volumes in 1925 and 1926. Its title translates to something like "My Struggle," and it is a combination of Hitler's autobiography and an exposition of his political ideology. It became a kind of textbook for the Nazi agenda.

new journalism: A school of journalism in the 1960s and 1970s that featured the use of literary techniques and devices in reporting. Tom Wolfe was its primary spokesman, and Truman Capote's *In Cold Blood* was one of its most famous achievements. Its most radical version was called gonzo journalism, in which the reporter participates so deeply in what he or she is reporting that he or she becomes the central figure of the piece. A notable example is Hunter Thompson's *Hell's Angels*.

Nietzschean superman: A concept associated with German philosopher Friedrich Nietzsche (1844–1900), for whom the *Übermensch* was a hypothetical but possible future being characterized by physical perfection—a capacity for power and a moral nature beyond good and evil.

pandit: In Hinduism, a scholar skilled in Sanskrit and Hindu law and religion.

poema: As the term is used by Gogol, it refers to a genre that falls halfway between an epic poem and a novel. He cites Cervantes's *Don Quixote* as an example, and it is what he called his own *Dead Souls*.

Rorschach test: An inkblot test developed by the Swiss psychologist Hermann Rorschach in which inkblots are perceived and interpreted by patients, and then their responses are analyzed to yield psychological insights. In *Watchmen*, the character known as Rorschach takes his name from the mask he wears, which resembles an inkblot whose pattern is always shifting.

utilitarianism: A philosophy, associated primarily with Jeremy Bentham and John Stuart Mill, that argues that usefulness is the primary moral criterion of action and that the greatest extent of human happiness determines the highest moral good—in epigrammatic terms, "the greatest good for the greatest number of people."

Biographical Notes

Bulgakov, Mikhail (1891–1940): A Russian dramatist, novelist, and short-story writer, Bulgakov was born in the Ukraine and was trained as a doctor, serving in that capacity in the Russian military in World War I—as well as with the White Army during the subsequent Russian Civil War. He moved to Moscow to become a full-time writer, where he quickly ran afoul of the new Soviet standards for art and ideology. After a series of successful plays, his work was more and more fiercely suppressed so that by the time he wrote *The Master and Margarita*—during the last 10 years of his life—he had no hope of seeing it in print in his own lifetime. At his death, he left the manuscript with his wife, Yelena Shilovskaya (the inspiration for Margarita in the novel), and she had to wait until 1966, during one of the Soviet "thaws," to get it published. The publication brought Bulgakov to the attention of the rest of the world; by now, a considerable body of his work is available outside of Russia.

Cisneros, Sandra (1954 –): A novelist, poet, and short-story writer, Cisneros was born in Chicago to a Mexican father and a Mexican-American mother. She was a student in the University of Iowa Writers' Workshop when she was inspired to write *The House on Mango Street* by her awareness of the differences between her own domestic experiences and those of her fellow students. The book took a long time to write, and it was published in 1983 by a Latino press in Texas. It was her second publication, the first having been a volume of poems published by another small press in San Jose, California. *The House on Mango Street* has since made its way into the mainstream and is now published by Random House. Regardless, it took her a long time to be able to live on the proceeds from her writing, and she held various jobs along the way to support herself. She has published a great deal more since *The House on Mango Street*, and she continues to live in San Antonio, Texas, still—as she says in the 1991 edition of the book—"as no man's wife and no man's mother." She has won numerous awards for her work.

Didion, Joan (1934 –): A novelist, essayist, dramatist, and (with her husband, John Gregory Dunne) screenwriter, Didion was born in Sacramento.

After moving around a great deal because her father was in the military, she settled back into the Sacramento area and graduated from the University of California, Berkeley. After college, she worked for two years at *Vogue* magazine, during which she wrote her first novel: *Run River*. Her first book of nonfiction was *Slouching towards Bethlehem* in 1968, although some of the essays had already appeared in periodicals. She has continued to produce a steady stream of well-crafted and beautifully written novels and books of nonfiction—as well as turned some of her own books into plays—and has received many awards for her writing. *The Year of Magical Thinking*, written in the period of mourning following her husband's death and published in 2003, is her most recent best seller.

Gibbons, Dave (1949–): An English artist and writer, Gibbons is best known for his artwork in *Watchmen*. He produced a considerable body of work for the British series *2000 AD* and for the *Doctor Who Weekly/Monthly*. By the mid-1980s, he was working for DC Comics. He also worked with Alan Moore on the Superman story "For the Man Who Has Everything." Since then, he has been writing and creating art and has helped produce computer games. He was also a consultant for the film version of *Watchmen*.

Gogol, Nikolai (1809–1852): A Russian novelist, short-story writer, and dramatist, Gogol was born in the Ukraine. He achieved fame with a collection of short stories based on life in the Ukraine (1831) and with his best-known work, the satirical play, *The Inspector General* (1836). For most of the rest of his life, he lived abroad, working on *Dead Souls*, which was published in 1842. It was intended as the first volume of a trilogy, but while working on a second part, Gogol began to be troubled spiritually, and he came to think that he was eternally damned. Convinced that his literary work was sinful, he destroyed two separate versions of Part II, only fragments of a draft of which survive. He is considered a precursor of realism in Russian literature and, thus, a forebear of Turgenev, Tolstoy, and Dostoevsky.

James, P. D. (1920–). Phyllis Dorothy James was born in Oxford. She finished secondary school but did not attend a university, going to work at age 16 in a variety of positions. Her husband returned from World War II a damaged man, so in 1949, James went to work for the National Health Services, providing much of the medical background she draws upon in her novels. After her husband's death in 1964, she worked in the Criminal Division of the British Home Office, becoming a specialist in juvenile delinquency. Again, her experience provided her with knowledge of criminal procedure and criminal behavior. She began her first book when she was 39, and *Cover Her Face* was immediately accepted for publication—she has never received a rejection notice. She has worked slowly but steadily over the years, so her longevity has allowed her to create a considerable body of work, almost all of it in the genre of crime or detective fiction.

Kushner, Tony (1956–): Raised in Lake Charles, Louisiana, Kushner attended Columbia University and New York University. After a series of early plays, he came to national attention with his two-play work *Angels in America*, produced in 1990 and 1991. The first, *Millennium Approaches*, won a Pulitzer Prize and was awarded a Tony Award as the best play of the year; the second, *Perestroika*, won another Tony Award for best play. Kushner continues to live in New York and continues his career as a playwright, in addition to being active as a lecturer and teacher.

Le Carré, John (1931–): The pen name of David Cornwell, British writer who attended school in Switzerland and Berne University before receiving his degree in modern languages from Oxford University in 1956. He was in military service in Austria and, after a couple of years of tutoring at Eton, joined the Foreign Service and was assigned to West Germany. Whether he was himself a spy is still an open question, and he has been ambiguous in his answers to the question, but his books are clearly based on some inside information about how the intelligence community works. *The Spy Who Came In from the Cold* was so successful that it allowed him to dedicate himself to writing after 1963, and many novels followed—some on cold war themes and some on subjects like international drug trafficking. His *The Constant Gardener* became a major motion picture. Graham Greene, somewhat of an expert in the field, wrote that *The Spy Who Came In from the Cold* was the best spy novel he had ever read.

Martel, Yann (1963–): Born in Spain to parents of French Canadian descent, Martel grew up in various places all over the world. After working at a variety of jobs, he started writing. His first two works received some warm critical praise but sold slowly. He went to India to work on his third novel, which was never written, but it is in India that he came up with the idea for Life of Pi, which was published in 2001. It made his reputation and won The Man Booker Prize in England, in addition to becoming an international best seller. Martel currently writes and teaches from his home base in Montreal, although he "lives internationally."

Moore, Alan (1953–): Moore was born into a working-class family in Northampton, England. After beginning as a cartoonist, he found work in the English comics industry, where he produced—among other things—the *V for Vendetta* series, which is set in a fascist and dystopian Britain. By 1983, he was working on the American series *Saga of the Swamp Thing*. In 1986, he wrote *Watchmen*, which—together with Frank Miller's *The Dark Knight*—redefined the comics medium and the concept of the costumed hero. *Watchmen* was the first-ever comic book recipient of the Hugo Award (for science fiction), and in 2005, *Time* magazine declared it one of the 100 best English-language novels since 1923. He continues to work on comic books and graphic novels, including some under his own imprint, America's Best Comics (ABC).

Orwell, George (1903–1950): The pseudonym of Eric Blair, English novelist and essayist. Orwell was born in India, was educated at Eton, and served with the Imperial Police in Burma from 1922 to 1927, an experience he loathed. He felt so guilty about his part in British colonialism that he spent many years thereafter trying to atone, an experience he often wrote about (see his famous and oft-anthologized "Shooting an Elephant," for example). His writing career was launched with *Down and Out in Paris and London*, and he became a well-known international figure as a political essayist and the author of such novels as *Animal Farm* (1945) and *Nineteen Eighty-Four* (1949). Throughout his writing career, he maintained independence from political affiliation and thought and was a critic of both Western and communist ideologies. Many of his essays are frequently anthologized and are still admired for their insight, clarity, and prescient anticipations of developments in the modern world.

Warren, Robert Penn (1905–1989): An American novelist, poet, and literary critic, Warren was born in Kentucky and was educated at Vanderbilt University; the University of California, Berkeley; Yale; and Oxford as a

Rhodes Scholar. He was also a member of the Fugitives with such eminent poets as John Crowe Ransom, Donald Davidson, and Allen Tate. With Cleanth Brooks, he edited *The Southern Review* and wrote, also with Brooks, perhaps the most influential textbook of their generation, *Understanding Poetry*, which promoted New Criticism as a method of literary analysis. He taught at Louisiana State University, the University of Minnesota, and Yale. A prolific novelist, poet, and author of literary essays, he received three Pulitzer Prizes during his lifetime (one for *All the King's Men* in 1946 and two for volumes of poetry). He became the United States's first Poet Laureate in 1986.

Zusak, Markus (1975–): An Australian novelist, Zusak was born to German immigrant working-class parents. He says that his parents' experiences have provided both the motivation and the subjects for much of his fiction to date, including at least the germ for *The Book Thief*, the book that established his international reputation and has won many awards.

Bibliography

Barley, Tony. *Taking Sides: The Fiction of John le Carré.* Philadelphia: Open University Press, 1986. A good analysis of *The Spy Who Came In from the Cold* that focuses on the author's ambivalent attitude toward Alec Leamas, whose progress in the novel moves through a procession of unresolved contradictions.

Bloom, Harold, ed. *Robert Penn Warren's "All the King's Men."* New York: Chelsea House, 1987. A collection of modern essays by various authors. All of them are useful, but see especially those by Arthur Mizener, Murray Krieger, Richard Gray, and Richard G. Law.

———. *Tony Kushner. Bloom's Modern Critical Views.* Philadelphia: Chelsea House, 2005. A collection of modern essays on the body of Kushner's work up to 2005. See especially the essay by Janelle Reinelt, which analyzes the extent to which Kushner's plays can be considered Brechtian epic theater.

Bohner, Charles. *Robert Penn Warren.* Rev. ed. Boston: Twayne, 1981. Like all of the books in the Twayne series, this is an overview of the author's life and all of his works. The analysis of *All the King's Men* is very helpful.

Bulgakov, Mikhail. *The Master and Margarita.* Translated by Diana Burgin and Katherine Tiernan O'Connor. New York: Vintage Books, 1995.

Chambers, Robert H., ed. *Twentieth Century Interpretations of "All the King's Men."* Englewood Cliffs, New Jersey: Prentice-Hall, 1977. A collection of essays by various authors on many aspects of Warren's novel. All of them are useful, but see especially the introduction by Chambers and the essay by James Ruoff.

Cisneros, Sandra. *The House on Mango Street.* New York: Vintage Books, 1989.

Cobbs, John L. *Understanding John le Carré*. Columbia: University of South Carolina Press, 1998. In his analysis of *The Spy Who Came In from the Cold*, Cobbs focuses on Alec Leamas's intellectual limitations, which set up the progress of the secondary plot: what Leamas learns and his development during the course of the novel.

Cullina, Alice. *ClassicNotes GradeSaver: "Life of Pi."* Rev. ed. by Damien Chazelle. Cambridge, MA: GradeSaver LLC, 2008. This book is designed to help students write papers on the novel, but it contains much useful information in the format of detailed plot analysis.

Curtis, J. A. E. *Bulgakov's Last Decade: The Writer as Hero*. New York: Cambridge University Press, 1987. A thorough analysis of Bulgakov's *The Master and Margarita*, focusing on three main topics: the relationship in the novel between Jerusalem and Moscow; Woland; and the Master, whom Curtis views as a romantic artist in contact with a higher truth.

Didion, Joan. *Slouching towards Bethlehem*. New York: Simon and Schuster, 1968.

Eagleton, Terry. *Literary Theory: An Introduction*. Minneapolis: University of Minnesota Press, 1983. This is a serious but accessible introduction to the complicated subject of literary theory. Its first chapter introduces the subject in a witty manner, and its definition of literature was used as a reference in this course.

Eysturoy, Annie O. *Daughters of Self-Creation: The Contemporary Chicana Novel*. Albuquerque: University of New Mexico Press, 1996. An insightful reading of the stories about women (particularly the Sally stories) and the ways in which writing helps Esperanza escape prescribed female roles and the achievement of identity in Cisneros's *The House on Mango Street*.

Felton, Sharon, ed. *The Critical Response to Joan Didion*. Westport, CT: Greenwood Press, 1994. In a volume of critical essays on Didion, see especially those by Evan Carton and Christ Anderson on her writing style and techniques.

Fingeroth, Danny. *The Rough Guide to Graphic Novels.* New York: Rough Guides, 2008. A good overview of the history of the genre, beginning with Richard Outcault's *Hogan's Alley* in 1895.

Fisher, James. *The Theater of Tony Kushner: Living Past Hope.* New York: Routledge, 2001. This book covers Kushner's body of work up to 2001. Its plot-summary analysis of *Angels in America* is very helpful.

Friedman, Ellen G., ed. *Joan Didion: Essays & Conversations.* Princeton, NJ: Ontario Review Press, 1984. A collection of essays on many aspects of Didion's career as an essayist and novelist. Also includes several informative interviews with the author.

Gardner, Averil. *George Orwell.* Boston: Twayne, 1987. Like all of the books in the Twayne series, this includes a brief biography and a survey of all of the author's major works. The background information and critical analysis of *Down and Out in Paris and London* are both very useful.

Gedez, Richard B. *P. D. James.* Boston: Twayne, 1986. An overview of James's life and works through *Innocent Blood.* Each novel is analyzed, and special attention is paid to the development of the characters of Adam Dalgliesh and Cordelia Gray from novel to novel.

Geis, Deborah R., and Steven F. Kruger, eds. *Approaching the Millennium: Essays on "Angels in America."* Ann Arbor: University of Michigan Press, 1997. Eighteen essays on various aspects of Kushner's plays. Kruger's essay on identity and conversion in the plays is especially insightful and provided much to the reading of the ending in Lecture 5.

Gibian, George, ed. *Nikolai Gogol: "Dead Souls." A Norton Critical Edition.* New York: W. W. Norton, 1985. Like others in the Norton Critical Edition series, this includes a complete text of the novel and a collection of essays—critical and biographical—on the work, some of them complete and some excerpted. The essays allow for many different perspectives on Gogol and his achievement.

Gogol, Nikolai. *Dead Souls: A Novel.* Translated by Richard Pevear and Larissa Volokhonsky. New York: Vintage Books, 1997.

Gravett, Paul. *Graphic Novels: Stories to Change Your Life.* London: Aurum Press, 2005. The parts of the book concerned with Alan Moore and *Watchmen* trace Moore's career and include an analysis of the novel, focusing on time, the linking of various plot strands, and some details of the graphic panels.

Gutiérrez-Jones, Leslie. "Different Voices: The Re-Bildung of the Barrio in Sandra Cisneros' *The House on Mango Street.*" In *Anxious Power: Reading, Writing, and Ambivalence in Narrative by Women,* edited by Carol J. Singley and Susan Elizabeth Sweeney, 295–312. Albany: State University of New York Press, 1993. Gutiérrez-Jones argues that in *The House on Mango Street,* Cisneros encroached on the male domains of Bildungsroman and Künstlerroman as Esperanza becomes a writer and redefines those genres.

Hammond, J. R. *A George Orwell Companion: A Guide to the Novels, Documentaries and Essays.* London: Macmillan, 1982. This book covers all of Orwell's works. Its treatment of the narrator's style and some of his techniques of presentation are very well explained and very helpful for readers in finding the tone of *Down and Out in Paris and London.*

Herbert, Marilyn, and Adina Herbert. *Book Club in a Box: "The Book Thief."* Toronto: Book Club in a Box, 2009. A guide designed, as the title suggests, for book club discussions of the novel. It includes such topics as characterization, themes, style and structure, and symbols.

Homberger, Eric. *John le Carré.* New York: Methuen, 1986. A good analysis of *The Spy Who Came In from the Cold* that argues that its central problem is the struggle to remain fully human in a society whose institutions have lost connection with individual feeling.

Hubly, Erlene. "The Formula Challenged: The Novels of P. D. James." *Modern Fiction Studies* 29, no. 3 (Autumn 1983): 511–521. A good account of the classical English crime novel, designed to show James's departures from and innovation upon the classic formula, using *The Black Tower* as illustration.

James, P. D. *Death of an Expert Witness.* New York: Warner Books, 1977.

———. *Shroud for a Nightingale.* New York: Simon and Schuster, 2001.

Kaveney, Roz. *Superheroes! Capes and Crusaders in Comics and Films.* New York: I. B. Tauris, 2008. A useful analytical plot summary is followed by insightful discussions of the title, the intercalary essays, and detailed character portraits of Rorschach and Adrian Veidt.

Kushner, Tony. *Angels in America. Part One: Millennium Approaches.* New York: Theatre Communications Group, 1993.

———. *Angels in America. Part Two: Perestroika.* New York: Theatre Communications Group, 1996.

Le Carré, John. *The Spy Who Came In from the Cold.* New York: Walker, 2005.

Lewis, Peter. *John le Carré.* New York: Frederick Ungar, 1985. A helpful compendium for the author's body of work up to 1985. Its analysis of *The Spy Who Came In from the Cold* focuses on the intellectual (moral and political) issues at the heart of the book. Many of its insights made their way into the lecture on the novel.

Martell, Yann. *Life of Pi.* New York: Harcourt, 2001.

McCracken, Ellen. "Sandra Cisneros' *The House on Mango Street*: Community-Oriented Introspection and the Demystification of Patriarchal Violence." In *Breaking Boundaries: Latina Writers and Critical Reading*, edited by Asunción Horno-Delgado et al, 62–71. Amherst: University of Massachusetts Press, 1989. McCracken addresses the ways in which Esperanza's escape is as much social as individualistic, and she discusses women's issues and the positive role models in the book.

Moore, Alan, and Dave Gibbons. *Watchmen.* New York: DC Comics, 2008.

Nagel, James. "Sandra Cisneros's *Cuentitos Latinos*: *The House on Mango Street.*" Chap. 4 in *The Contemporary American Short-Story Cycle: The Ethnic Resonance of Genre*. Baton Rouge: Louisiana State University, 2001. Good readings of most of the stories in Cisneros's *The House on Mango Street* that focus on the themes of houses, writing, gender roles, and Esperanza's religious heritage.

Natov, Nadine. *Mikhail Bulgakov.* Boston: Twayne, 1985. An overview of the author's life and works. Includes a helpful reading of *The Master and Margarita*, whose thesis, she argues, is that "nothing can prevent the human mind from escaping the banality of everyday life into the realm of the supernatural."

Nielsen, Ken. *Tony Kushner's "Angels in America."* New York: Continuum, 2008. A helpful reading of the plays and a consideration of Kushner's debt to Brecht's epic theater.

Orwell, George. *Down and Out in Paris and London.* New York: Harcourt, 1961.

Reynolds, Richard. *Super Heroes: A Modern Mythology.* Jackson: University Press of Mississippi, 1992. A detailed analysis of *Watchmen*, particularly insightful in the ways it uses older comic books and traditions in order to become "a fairly systematic critique of the development of the superhero genre in sequential art."

Setchkarev, Vsevolod. *Gogol: His Life and Works.* Translated by Robert Kramer. New York: New York University Press, 1965. As the title suggests, this is an overview of Gogol as a person and writer, in a reader-friendly style and format. The analysis of *Dead Souls* is thorough and insightful and includes an analysis of the fragmentary Part II.

Siebenheller, Norma. *P. D. James.* New York: Frederick Ungar, 1981. Good analyses of all of James's novels through *Innocent Blood.* After treating each novel individually, Siebenheller treats the body of work topically: "Law and Justice," "Major Themes," "Major Characters," and "A Sense of Style."

Warren, Robert Penn. *All the King's Men*. New York: Bantam, 1968.

Weeks, Laura D., ed. *"The Master and Margarita": A Critical Companion*. Evanston, IL: Northwestern University Press, 1996. A collection of essays on various aspects of Bugakov's novel. Weeks's introduction argues for the possibility of Ivan as the single source for the narration.

Weingarten, Marc. *The Gang That Wouldn't Write Straight: Wolfe, Thompson, Didion, and the New Journalism Revolution*. New York: Crown, 2006. An account of the new journalism movement of the 1960s and 1970s that focuses on the writers in the title (plus some others) but also traces the movement's roots back to such authors as Jonathan Swift, Charles Dickens, and George Orwell, all of whom used literary techniques in what is essentially journalism—a distinguishing characteristic of the writers featured in Weingarten's book.

Winchell, Mark Royden. *Joan Didion*. Boston: Twayne, 1989. In a book that covers all aspects of Didion's career, there are some fine detailed analyses of many of the essays in *Slouching towards Bethlehem* and *The White Album*.

Wright, A. Colin. *Mikhail Bulgakov: Life and Interpretations*. Buffalo, NY: University of Toronto Press, 1978. A thorough reading of *The Master and Margarita* whose thesis is that the novel is concerned with the conflict between the spiritual and the material world—a thesis, Wright argues, that underlies all of Bulgakov's works.

Zusak, Markus. *The Book Thief*. New York: Alfred A. Knopf, 2007.

Internet Resources

"The New Yorker" Book Club Blog. http://www.newyorker.com/online/blogs/bookclub/down-and-out-in. A long-running blog by various critics and writers on the question of the truth of the experiences narrated in George Orwell's *Down and Out in Paris and London* from a variety of points of

view and assessments with some careful and intelligent discussion of what difference it makes.

Schmoop. "The Book Thief." http://www.shmoop.com/book-thief/. A user-friendly analysis of Zusak's novel, divided into various topics that cover most of the important aspects of the novel. Be prepared to spend some time with this site, enlivened by the wit of the analysts.

Schmoop. "Life of Pi." http://www.shmoop.com/life-of-pi/. Like the Shmoop site about *The Book Thief*, this one is designed to help high school and college students prepare for examinations and write essays on the novel. It, too, contains abundant information on the novel and is charming in its presentation.

Credit

Music supplied by Getty Images.

Notes

Notes

Notes

Notes

Notes

Notes

Notes

Notes